D.B. Cooper Where are You

My Own Story

D.B. Cooper

On Thanksgiving Eve, 1971, in driving wind and freezing rain, a man calling himself Dan Cooper was clutching a bag filled with $200,000 in stolen cash when he parachuted into the night and disappeared. Cooper bailed out of the hijacked Northwest Airlines' jet somewhere just north of Portland, Oregon. Over time the mystery of legendary folk hero D.B. Cooper has continued and grown. Now, Walter Grant tells all in a fictionalized autobiography.

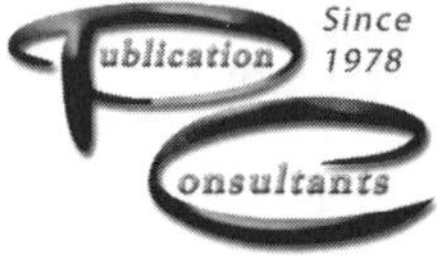

PO Box 221974 Anchorage, Alaska 99522-1974
books@publicationconsultants.com
www.publicationconsultants.com

ISBN 978-1-59433-076-6
Library of Congress Catalog Card Number: 2008927631

—First Edition—

Dedicated to:
Carmon and Crystal;
You survived the seventies,
I'm proud of you.

A special thanks to:
Bob
Joe
Lyle
Terry
Claude

Manufactured in the United States of America.

Contents

Prologue

There are movies and documentaries about me. Books and songs have been written about me. Numerous articles have appeared in newspapers and magazines about me. Several people claimed to have known me while others have actually claimed to be me.

Many theories are floating around: some say I bailed out over Lake Oswego, Oregon, which accounts for money turning up in the Columbia River. Some say I'm at the bottom of Lake Merwin. Others believe I jumped 30 miles north of Portland, Oregon and walked back to my home in Woodland, Washington where I still live today. One FBI agent even claims he killed me when he shot another man.

I am getting on in years and have decided it is time to set the record straight and tell my own story. The decision did not come easily; part of me wants to keep the mystery alive and leave everyone to their own conclusions. We are all aware of the difficulty of keeping a secret, even when it is in our own best interest. Emotional weakness finally won out over logic.

By telling my own story I have nothing to gain and everything to lose—my freedom, a beautiful and loving wife, and a comfortable, if not luxurious, lifestyle in a peaceful part of the country. The FBI charged me with hijacking Northwest Orient flight 305 the day before the statute of limitations ran out, so a warrant for my arrest is still on the books and can, and I suspect will, be served if and when I am found.

What I hope to-do by telling my own story is to alert youngsters to how a single stupid, spur-of-the-moment decision can snowball and lead downhill to the point of no return. Through a near-death experience I was able to turn my life around, and although I live comfortably I am not free. I am a wanted man constantly looking over my shoulder.

DB Cooper

A Taste of Candi

The sun was hanging only a few degrees above the jagged peaks of the Kohala Mountains by the time I reached the narrow strip of sand separating the jungle from the Pacific Ocean—evening was on its way, with night not far behind. I stopped in a dense area of palms and deposited my last load of bricks inside a wooden crate with the rest of the bags, and then replaced the palm fronds to camouflage the box before heading for the beach.

It had been a long day and I was ready for some rest and relaxation. The relaxation I had in mind had just caught a wave about 30 yards out—waves broke close to shore in this little cove. Candi was a sun worshiper with long black hair and was often mistaken for a local. Her evenly tanned body, glowing golden in the lingering rays of sunlight as she slipped her board along the face of the wave, was a testament to her love of nature and disdain for swimsuits. As I watched her work the wave, I wondered what I would have been doing, where I would have been, and what my life would have been like had that fateful meeting which seemed like only yesterday, but in reality was a lifetime ago never occurred. She spotted me and headed toward the beach. When the wave petered out she eased herself into the water and waded ashore, walked up the beach to within 3 feet of where I sat, dropped her board onto the sand and slowly sank to her knees. Her eyes sparkled as she asked, "You tired?"

"Not that tired," I answered.

That devilish little smile I had come to know so well played across her lips as she arched her body and leaned backward. Tilting her head even further back she brought both arms up and while reaching behind her head gathered up her hair and gave it a couple of twists before bringing it around in front of her. She gave it a few more twists to squeeze out the water, and then leaning forward, let go of her hair, shook it loose and as she straightened up, tossed her head, flipping the hair behind her back. This exhibition had nothing to do with drying her hair, it was all for my pleasure. Candi knew I delighted in visually exploring her body and indulged me at every opportunity.

As evening fell, I leaned back on my elbows and while my eyes played slowly across her curvaceous silhouette my thoughts drifted back to the first time I glimpsed Candi's exquisite body; the moment and image had been burned for all eternity into the ferrite cores of my brain.

Candi was the type of girl young men's mothers warn them about and pray their sons will never bring home for Sunday dinner—she was also the type of girl young men hope to encounter and experience at least once before they become old men. The moment I laid eyes on her I knew she was trouble, but the pleasures she offered far outweighed the many perils that would surely follow. During those few brief seconds when our eyes met and locked, invitations and promises were exchanged and understood without the benefit of words or gestures. Oh yeah, she was trouble, but I didn't care, she was the woman of my dreams and she was about to make all my fantasies come true. Little did I know that similar thoughts were running through her mind. She had dreams and fantasies of her own, but her dreams and fantasies went far beyond what I could have ever imagined.

She was dancing in a topless bar on Tacoma's seedy south side, a noisy, smoke-filled dive frequented by hard-drinking GIs from nearby Fort Lewis. Everyone had their reason for spending Saturday night in one of the shabbiest places on the strip. Some, with no place to go and nothing to do, were there out of habit—others were there searching for their own dreams and fantasies, which they hoped to discover with the next round but in their hearts knew would never materialize. A few lifers were there to recall the good old days that lay hidden in the bottle on its way to their table. Me, I was there to get stinking, lousy, passed-out-on-the-floor drunk. Tomorrow morning, with blurry vision, a splitting headache, and a busted wallet I would board a Tan Son Nhut-bound C-141 Starlifter at McCord Air Force Base. But all that was forgotten when the spotlights focused my attention on the exotic Candi undulating sensuously on a small stage in the center of the smoke-filled room. What I didn't know was that my life was about to change forever.

I was heading for a table in a rear corner where I wasn't likely to be disturbed—only serious drinkers sat at rear tables in a topless bar on amateur night—and was just passing the stage when the spotlights came on. When I looked up I found myself staring into two dark, bewitching eyes that in one brief moment looked into the depths of my very soul and read my every thought. Our minds merged, our thinking became a single process and in that one fleeting moment she burned her dreams and desires into my subconsciousness.

An hour ago getting drunk was the only thing I had been thinking about—now it was the furthest thing from my mind. I pulled a pack of Raleighs from the front pocket of my denim jacket and, performing a ritual practiced since I was a teenager, tore off the corner of the pack and banged it against my finger until a cigarette popped out about an inch, then held the pack to my mouth and slowly pulled it away, leaving the cigarette dangling between my lips. I tossed the pack of Raleighs on the table and using only one hand, removed a book of matches from the same front pocket of my denim jacket, opened the cover, pushed a single match away from the rest of the matches, closed the cover, bent the match in half and forced the head of the match across the striking strip with my thumb. I waited until the initial flare of the ignited match died down, then touched my cigarette to the flame. After filling my lungs with smoke and without removing the cigarette from my mouth, I blew out the match and then, still using only one hand, tore off the spent match, dropped it into the ash tray, and tossed the matchbook onto the table beside the Raleighs. I filled my lungs with smoke again, let a generous amount of Wild Turkey trickle down my throat, leaned back, blew a smoke ring at the ceiling, and waited. I knew the wait wouldn't be long, but already it seemed like an eternity. I watched anxiously as she approached and slipped into the chair directly opposite me. Her eyes sparkled and a devilish smile played across her lips as she asked, "What brings a nice boy like you to a place like this?"

The flimsy robe left little to the imagination. I let another swig of Wild Turkey lie on my palate for a few seconds before allowing it to ooze past my gullet, then leaned forward resting my elbows on the table and waited a few seconds to give my answer more impact, "Naughty girls like you."

We were both being kind in referring to one another with the boy and girl routine; she was in her late twenties and I had just celebrated my thirty-first birthday.

While pretending to be unaware her robe had fallen open, she invited me to look inside as she leaned across the table and placed her elbows only a couple of inches away from mine and asked, "Do you think I'm a naughty girl?"

I accepted her invitation and tilted my head to emphasize the point of staring inside her open robe long enough to make my intentions obvious, then slowly brought my eyes back up to meet her inquisitive stare and let a smile, which I hoped was as devilish as hers, play across my own lips for several seconds before I finally answered, "I certainly hope so."

She feigned an attempt to pull the robe closed and said, "Well, now that we've got that out of the way, what's your name?"

"D. B. Cooper, what's yours?"

"Candice Jackson, but my friends call me Candi. What's DB stand for?"

"Nothing."

"Nothing? I've never heard of anybody not having a name."

"I've got a name, it's DB "

I guess I sounded a bit irritated because she lowered her voice and said, "I didn't mean to offend you; it's just that I've never met anyone with an initial name."

I lifted my hands off the table a few inches and turned them palms up in one of those it-ain't-no-big-thing gestures everyone interprets as "It's okay." She looked at me for a couple of seconds, leaned forward and let that mischievous little smile play across her lips for several seconds. "Oh, come on, it has to stand for something. Why didn't your parents give you a real name?"

I leaned forward as though I was about to divulge some earthshaking secret and asked, "Do you really want to know?"

"Well," she hesitated for a moment and shrugged. "You've got to admit, it's not every day you run into someone with just letters for a name."

I leaned even closer until my face was only inches from hers, lowered my voice to a whisper and asked, "Do you promise to never bring it up again?"

She put her right hand up even with her face, placed her left hand above her heart and said, "I promise."

"You won't tell anyone?"

"Never."

"Cross your heart and hope to die?" She made a big X on her chest and repeated the phrase, "Cross my heart and hope to die."

"Okay, I'll tell you."

I took in a deep breath and let it out slowly, looked around in all directions, as though I was making sure no one was close enough to hear and then leaned forward and in a voice, meant to sound as though I was embarrassed said, "Shortly after I was born and my mother was holding me for the first time, a nurse looked at me and said, 'What a darling baby,' and from that moment on my mother called me D.B for darling baby. Later, when the doctor asked what name to put on the birth certificate, my mother answered without hesitation, 'D. B. Cooper.'"

For a moment I could have sworn Candi's eyes misted over. She sighed, reached across, placed her hand on mine and, in a tender voice whispered, "That's just about the sweetest story I've ever heard."

"Well, don't go around repeating it, okay?"

"I'll never mention it again."

As a waitress approached, Candi stated in a hushed voice, "If you don't buy me a drink I'll have to sit at another table, it's a house rule," adding quickly, "I don't want to sit at another table."

She looked at me with big sad eyes and pleaded, "Will you buy me a drink?"

I knew I wasn't the first guy to hear that line, but it didn't matter; I was playing my own game. It's the same all over the world, people in bars play games. It's to be expected. It's part of the scene. I had no doubt Candi was very good at games. "Sure, I'll buy you anything you want. What do you want?"

She hesitated for only a moment before saying, "Another life."

Her eyes were pleading and I knew she was serious when she asked, "D. B. Cooper, will you buy me another life?"

The period for small talk had ended; it was time to cut to the chase, so I pushed my advantage.

"You already know the question I'm about to ask, don't you?"

"Sure. You want to know what's in it for you, so go ahead and ask."

She had gone way beyond her regular game of hustling drinks and I had no doubt she was dead serious about wanting a new life and had already decided, long before approaching my table, that I was her ticket. "Okay, what's in it for me?"

"All the things you dream about and things you never imagined."

Even if I'd wanted to refuse her offer it would have been impossible, but I had no intention of refusing. I was eager to accept. I had no doubt she was a witch and had cast a spell over me, but it didn't matter—I had gone under it willingly.

"Candice Jackson, you just got yourself a new life."

The waitress carefully laid out two little cocktail napkins and then placed another double shot of Wild Turkey in front of me, and a rum and coke, which I knew was all coke, in front of Candi—girls hustling in bars rarely get alcohol in their drinks. When I dropped a double sawbuck on the serving tray and told the waitress to keep the change she gave me a big smile along with the automatic thank you, and glanced at Candi with a raised eyebrow—I knew with a tip that size she got the message and wouldn't interrupt us again. For the next twenty minutes I nursed my whiskey while we exchanged thumbnail accounts of our past lives. I didn't know how much, if anything, of what she was telling me was the truth, and I wondered if she suspected me of lying to her. My guess was she believed every word, if for no other reason than that she wanted to believe me.

Lying came easy for me, I had been lying since I left home and took pride in being able to fabricate a story, on the spot, about anything and everything and convince people it was the gospel. I don't know why I'd lied about my name and wondered what she would have said had she known DB was short for dirt bag, a name hung on me by Drill Instructor Cooper in basic training. Using D. B. Cooper as a bar game alias was just my way of taking a shot at my old drill instructor. Lying seemed the thing to do in the beginning and now, as one lie led to another, and plans were being made for the rest of the night, it seemed unwise to change horses in midstream. Initially I had figured on a one-night stand in which lying, on both sides, was part of the game, but planning had rapidly expanded to include tomorrow and before long we were talking about next week, then Christmas and News Year's Eve. Suddenly I realized I was just as serious about the planning and scheming as Candi and I knew I wouldn't be on board the big C-141 cargo plane, transporting my unit to Saigon, when it lifted off from McCord Air Force Base.

I would be listed as AWOL and with my unit on its way to Viet Nam, I would probably be listed as a deserter as well. This being the case, it would be safer for me if Candi knew nothing about me or my past. My lies would be her truth. This way there would be no chance of her giving me away either accidentally or, should things not turn out the way she envisioned, on purpose. However, the most important reason, at the moment, for continuing the lie was to make sure I got a taste of Candi.

Covering the Bases

Every event in my life seemed to start with, end with, and evolve around a woman. Fairy tales all started with "Once upon a time"—chapters of my life began with, "There was this girl." I took a bite of my hamburger, popped a French fry into my mouth, and thought about the past few hours. I couldn't believe I was going AWOL. And for what, a few nights in a bar girl's bed? Either I had lost what little sanity I ever possessed or she was, indeed, a witch. It didn't matter now, it was too late to be having second thoughts. I had gone far beyond the point of no return and was doomed to whatever fate awaited me. I only hoped I'd covered all the bases.

Now that our plans, born out of coincidence and emotion, were established and set firmly in hope and promise, I set out to take care of some loose ends. If I was to be successful in shedding my old identity and becoming D. B. Cooper I had to create a series of circumstances that would be at least a diversion and hopefully convincing enough to anyone investigating my disappearance to conclude I was dead.

Any military town or city seems to have more than its share of unscrupulous people who make a habit out of preying on GIs. Many of these people are in the automobile repair business. I decided to make their greed and dishonesty work to my advantage. I knew money was going to be a problem until I could get myself reestablished, and although I had cashed my army paycheck earlier in the day and still had the money in my pocket, I wanted to put my hands on as much cash as possible within the next couple of hours. GIs always seemed to need money and word of where to go and who to see when this need arises circulated regularly in the military community. I stopped at one such establishment, and using my Chevron card purchased four of the most expensive tires I could buy. With mounting, balancing, and road hazard insurance the bill came to a little over four hundred dollars. However, the guy didn't put the tires on my car—he gave me three hundred dollars in cash. The difference went into the attendant's pocket, not the owner's cash register. I used my Union 76 card to make a similar deal at another gas station. My BankAmericard was almost maxed out and only netted me a hundred bucks, but counting the cash left from my paycheck I now had more than twelve hundred dollars in cold hard cash.

I drove to a supermarket parking lot and took all the money out of my wallet, put five twenty-dollar bills in each of the two front pockets on my denim jacket, slipped off my boots, divided the rest of the money equally, pushed it down into the bottom of my socks, then pulled my boots on again. The first part of my plan had gone as well as could be expected. Now came the critical part.

I pulled out of the parking lot and headed toward an area of town where anyone alone and on foot this time of night could easily find himself in harm's way. I drove around until I located a bus stop. According to the schedule, the next bus was due in about twenty-five minutes. I drove back to a bar I had spotted earlier. The only light to be seen, outside of a Coors's sign over the door, was shining on a sign that read "Warm beer, cold sandwiches, and no GoGo Girls." I parked in back, left my wallet on the seat, the keys in the ignition, hung my dog tags on the mirror, and walked back to the bus stop. It wasn't a matter of whether or not someone took my car or tried to use my credit cards, it was a matter of when they took it and when they tried to charge something on my BankAmericard. It would be thirty days before the army turned my case over to the civilian authorities. It wouldn't take long for them to find my car; whoever was driving it would have a hard time explaining how he came by the car, why he had tried to use my credit cards, and what happened to me. Obviously, I was already missing and, with luck, would be written off as dead, a victim of foul play—a reasonable conclusion, considering the circumstances.

The bus was on schedule and almost empty. No one got off and I was the only one waiting to get on. About a dozen stops later I spotted a telephone at an all-night gas station across the street and exited the bus by the rear door. At the gas station I called a taxi, which took me back to South Tacoma and dropped me off at a twenty-four-hour diner.

I had finished my hamburger, started on a second order of French fries and was beginning to wonder why Candi hadn't shown up as promised. Could it be she was having second thoughts? I didn't think so. I stared out the window and found myself, once again, questioning my intelligence, or more appropriately, my lack of common sense. I wondered where I'd be and what I'd be doing had I never left Texas.

Small-town girls can light up a young cowboy's life on Saturday night and ranch life has its moments, but when all is said and done ranching is a lot of hard work and for a nineteen-year-old just out of high school, a very dull life. As summer came to an end and most of my friends went off to college, I had felt a need to get out of Texas. A navy recruiter provided the opportunity.

The recruiter's words "Join the Navy and see the world," were music to the ears of a small-town kid from west Texas and two days later my parents drove me into Plainview, where I caught a bus to Lubbock. From Lubbock a train took me across New Mexico, Arizona, and California into the very heart of San Diego, a city perched on the edge of the Pacific Ocean. A couple of Shore Patrol met me and the dozen or so other recruits and herded us onto a bus for a short trip along Harbor Drive to the Naval Training Center. It was a beautiful city of blue water and green hills. The breeze, unlike the hot, dry winds of the Texas plains, was warm and pleasant. I knew I'd made the right decision.

After boot camp I was assigned to a destroyer at Subic Bay in the Philippine Islands. The "old salts" always got a kick out of taking a young sailor on his first liberty in a foreign port. I will only say my first liberty in Olongapo was a night I will never forget. P.I. bar girls were reminiscent of the New Orleans girl Dylan sang about—they not only knew what you needed, they knew what you wanted. They also knew what they wanted—what they wanted was a ticket to America. Within a year and just shortly before my ship was to return to her home port in San Diego, I found myself married to an Olongapo bar girl. I moved her into an apartment in National City while my ship was in rework at the Ship Repair Facility at the Thirty-second Street naval station. After refitting, we went on a three-month shakedown cruise to MIDPAC (Middle Pacific). When we pulled into port at Pearl Harbor and liberty call sounded I headed for Honolulu and a Hotel Street bar with a couple of shipmates. We struck up a conversation with a sailor off the USS *Kitty Hawk*. The new super carrier (CV 63) was home based in San Diego and was deploying to WESTPAC (western Pacific). When we started talking about "Diego" not being much of a liberty town, he told us about his wild weekend with a girl he'd met at the Westerner in National City and showed us a snapshot of a girl scantily clad in nothing but black lingerie. It was a picture of my wife.

My marriage and my tour of duty with the navy ended at about the same time. All I had to show for my four years in the navy was an old army surplus Harley-Davidson motorcycle and about three hundred dollars in the bottom of my sock. I went back to Texas to see my parents and hung around for a week. A week was all I could take; my hometown was now more boring than ever. I headed back to the West coast figuring I'd look for work and when I had a little money saved up, take advantage of my GI Bill and go to college. When I got back to San Diego I ran into a couple of ex-swabbie biking buddies I'd known at Thirty-second Street. They told me there was good money to be earned working the canneries in Alaska. My old buddies were heading out the next day and invited me to come along. With nothing better to do I accepted.

We spent almost every day that summer working long hours in the canneries on Kodiak Island, but we were well rewarded. With our pockets full of hundred-dollar bills we sold our bikes and flew back to Seattle, where we said farewell and went our separate ways. With winter coming on and money burning a hole in my pocket, I bought a new Harley-Davidson Duo-glide and with no particular destination in mind, headed south.

The counterculture was well underway in California and kids with backpacks had their thumbs out all along Highway 101—I was twenty-four years old and considered anyone under eighteen a kid. However, mixed in with the jail bait were lots of girls of legal age looking for adventure. Somewhere in the redwoods north of San Francisco I hooked up with a runaway from south-side Chicago. She stayed with me until early spring when my money ran out—no money, no honey.

I sold my bike, thinking I would go back to Kodiak and work the canneries again and planned to use some of the money to buy a used bike when it was time to leave. A month latter I was ready to head out, but I had already spent most of the money I'd got for my Harley—easy come, easy go—and still hadn't bought a used motorcycle, and the seventy-five dollars I had left weren't going to buy me a bike that would get me out of the state, much less to Alaska. I figured hitchhiking was my only option when, as fate would have it, coming out of a bar on West Broadway I spotted a new full-dress Harley-Davidson Electra-glide parked in front of the Seven Seas Locker Club. There stood my ticket to ride. I could travel the Alcan in style, pick up some easy money by selling the Harley in Anchorage, take the train to Seward and from there, catch the ferry to Kodiak. The more I thought about it the better it sounded. I figured by staying east of the Sierra and the Cascades I'd make better time. I also reasoned the cops would be looking for a stolen motorcycle along the coast, not in the desert, so I headed out of San Diego on Highway 395. I didn't even make it out of the state—I made it only a few miles past Lone Pine. The brakes left a lot to be desired, but otherwise the Electro-glide was true to its name. At 90 miles per hour I barely felt the road. A highway patrolman, riding a Harley of his own, was impressed with my bike and sympathetic to a fellow biker tempted with, as he put it, a fine machine, to exceed the speed limit on a deserted highway at three in the morning and might have let me off with a warning had I been able to produce the motorcycle registration card.

Twelve months in Vacaville didn't change my destination; it merely set me back a year. Since there were not a lot of things to spend money on in prison, cigarettes were my biggest expense, I still had almost twenty dollars when I started hitchhiking north on Highway 99 the following spring. A dozen or so rides and a couple of weeks later a trucker picked me up near Medford, Oregon and suggested it would probably be winter by the time I hitchhiked to Kodiak and advised me to seek work with the timber industry. I was still set on going to Alaska, but another week passed before I finally crossed the bridge between Portland, Oregon and Vancouver, Washington. I was beginning to give serious consideration to the trucker's suggestion when an empty log truck pulled onto the highway heading north. I flagged him down—truckers were always pretty good about giving rides. He had just dropped his logs off where they would be loaded onto a barge on the Colombia River and was returning for another load. When I inquired about the possibility of getting a job with one of the timber companies the driver chuckled and asked if I could handle a dangerous job requiring hard work and long hours with low pay. When I said I could handle it if the pay wasn't too low, he said he might be able to help me. The trucker dropped me off at one of Weyerhaeuser's yards and told me to see the yarder engineer who went by the name Big Jim and I should mention his name, Curly. I surmised the name Curly was some sort of a joke—the trucker was as bald as an eagle.

The first couple of days I worked with a choker setter called Stubbs learning how to hook logs onto the high lead, and on the third day I was on my own. Dragging a 30-foot-long choker cable weighing 60 pounds through the brush was physically demanding, and the job didn't pay nearly as well as the canneries, but it was a lot more interesting than lopping the heads off salmon and pulling their guts out. The logging industry, for the most part, like the canneries, shut down in the winter months. I liked working in the woods and spent most of my time off hiking or fishing. The only downside for a kid from the Texas Panhandle was the rain and overcast skies. It wasn't uncommon to go a week without sunshine. By November, when Weyerhaeuser began shutting down operations, I wasn't just ready; I was way beyond ready to get out of the rain and mud. I was tired of looking at overcast skies and was eager to find a place where the sun was shining and the sky was blue. When a fellow choker setter named Krocker suggested we team up and head south, along the coast, in his Volkswagen van, I accepted his offer without hesitation.

Since neither of us had been concerned about getting haircuts, shaving, or buying new clothes while in the woods we looked pretty much like any other hippie on the road. With the Volkswagen van and a supply of marijuana—Krocker grew his own—we were accepted by the counterculture as one of their own.

After spending six months in the woods, the mixture of free love, marijuana parties, and cheap wine was just what we were looking for. The young hippie girls were willing to provide the free love as long as we had wine and marijuana. As the weather grew cooler, we moved farther south. Highway 1, from Monterey to Morro Bay, was one big party, but since everyone had the same idea, heading south to warmer weather, the beaches were getting overcrowded. So we headed to Mexico with a couple of eighteen-year-old girls we picked up at one of the beach parks south of Los Angeles—they told us they were eighteen, we didn't ask for proof.

We spent the rest of the winter either spaced out or drunk, sometimes both, on the beaches in Baja, mostly between Rosarito and Ensenada. When our money started getting short, the girls took up with a couple of other guys, but by then we had grown tired of them and didn't consider them much of a loss. We pooled our resources and figured we had enough money to have one last night in Tijuana and get back to our jobs in Washington State with a few dollars still in our pockets. Tijuana turned out to be a big mistake.

Krocker had just parked the Volkswagen when a Mexican pulled up in a rusted-out old car with dents all over it and accused Krocker of running into him and demanded he pay two hundred dollars or he would call the cops. Krocker flipped him the bird and told him to get lost—an argument ensued and Krocker decked the guy. The next thing I knew the police were hauling Krocker off to jail and the guy who accused Krocker of running into him was towing away the Volkswagen. I got the hell out of there and hoofed it across the border as fast as I could. As far as I know Krocker is still in a Mexican prison.

I got my old job back with Weyerhaeuser and about a month later the yarder engineer moved me from choker setter to hook tender. My second year of logging was pretty much the same as the first—hard work, long hours, and low pay, but by the end of the season I had enough money to buy another motorcycle. The Japanese had started selling a trail bike which had the advantage of being street legal. The Yamaha 360 Induro was the perfect bike for me and couldn't have come at a better time because I not only had taken over cultivation of Krocker's old marijuana patches but I'd planted over twenty of my own—I figured if Krocker showed up I'd share them all, but if he didn't then it wouldn't matter. Every Sunday, on my day off, I hiked along the old logging roads until I found a suitable spot and put in a few seeds. Now with the off-road bike I could keep a closer eye on my plants and not spend most of my time hiking from one patch to another.

The owner of a big brewery once replied, when asked how much of his product he drank, "Whiskey is for selling, not drinking." I made that my policy. I'd learned how easy it was to blow your wad on booze, drugs, and women and even though we didn't buy our dope since Krocker had a good supply of home-grown marijuana, it still contributed to my being broke when I got back to my job.

My first crop was pretty good, but since I was new to the trade I didn't make much money. I met a couple of guys who had grown pot on federal lands for several years and they gave me a crash course in the art of growing and marketing marijuana. The next year I planted my seeds in makeshift hothouses and then transplanted the seedlings throughout Weyerhaeuser's property in areas already logged; these areas wouldn't be revisited by loggers for several years. By harvest time I had a well-camouflaged drying shed a short distance from each patch; I also designed and built a portable device for compressing the stripped and dried marijuana leaves into bricks (small bales).

For every dollar I made logging I made twenty selling marijuana; I had found my calling. I didn't show up looking for a job with Weyerhaeuser the following spring, but instead went into marijuana growing full time and realized an even better year. However, things were beginning to change in the marijuana industry. I lost 20 percent of my crop to poachers, and besides poachers I had to contend with Drug Enforcement Agency spotter aircraft. To make matters worse, Weyerhaeuser had their own people wandering through the woods searching for marijuana plants. Still, even with these problems I made over two hundred thousand dollars. The following year promised to be the best yet, but after getting shot at by a couple of poachers I started packing a thirteen-shot, 9-millimeter Browning automatic with a couple of extra clips. A few weeks later when a shootout with what I thought was another poacher left a DEA agent dead I decided it was time to get out of the pot-farming business. I knew it wouldn't be long before the authorities would be looking for whoever shot the federal agent and figured it was time to get out of Dodge. Very few people knew I was farming marijuana and the ones who knew weren't going to tell the Feds; still, I didn't intend to be around when they started asking questions. The trick was to disappear without a trace or at worst, disappear without leaving an easy trail to follow. I rode into Woodland where I rented an apartment, knocked on the door of my landlord, informed him I had an emergency in the family and would be leaving for Phoenix, Arizona early the next morning and would be giving up my apartment. I paid him an extra hundred dollars in addition to forfeiting my security deposit and money I'd paid for rent, to clean up and dispose of whatever I left in the apartment, which would be everything I wasn't wearing when I left. I fixed myself a couple of sandwiches before setting my alarm, taking a shower, and going to bed. It was just after midnight when the alarm woke me. I put on a pot of coffee before I began dressing. Two cups of coffee and a couple of doughnuts later I closed and locked the door behind me, before I quietly walked my dirt bike out into the street, and push-started it. With the aid and unauthorized use of a rowboat I dumped the Yamaha in a deep area of Merwin Lake and threw the pistol in behind it. I left the boat exactly where I'd found it, and walked back into Woodland, where I caught the first bus to Tacoma. I bought a canvas tote bag before walking to the bank and emptying my safe deposit boxes, and then walked back to the bus station and caught the next bus to Seattle. A taxi dropped me at pier 49. I walked into the Alaska Marine Highway Office and bought a ticket on the next ferry to Alaska. Luckily it was leaving that afternoon. I paid for passage to Haines, but got off in Juneau, where I bought a change of clothes, a few personal items, and another tote bag before getting a room at the Bergmann. After a not-so-good night's sleep, I caught a taxi to the airport and purchased round-trip fare to Los Angeles in the name of Daniel Burke—I had no intention of using the return ticket. In Los Angeles I paid for a round-trip ticket to San Diego using the name Danny Baxter. I needed a few days to rest, to get my head together and make plans, so I checked into the El Cortez Hotel under the name Dan Burton. I stayed in my room except to eat and check train schedules. I decided Texas would be as safe as any place and three days later I climbed aboard an eastbound train at the same Santa Fe station where, thirteen years before, as a kid still wet behind the ears, I had first stepped onto California's terra firma. Since I had grown up in the Panhandle, I figured it best to avoid that part of the Lone Star state and decided El Paso would be a good place to kick back and reevaluate my life. If someone started asking too many questions I could always slip across the river to Juarez.

After almost five years in the Northwest, I was waterlogged and welcomed the bright sun, blue skies, and the dry west Texas wind. It felt good to be home. The first two things on my agenda were to pig out on Tex-Mex and round up some decent clothes. I was tired of the "Beat Generation" look and had a hankering to get back to my Texas roots. I satiated my appetite at La Paloma Blanca and at El Paso Saddle and Blanket Company I bought six pairs of Levis, a good leather belt, two denim jackets, a dozen shirts, a black beaver felt range rider and a new pair of Justin boots. I slipped into my new duds and for a moment or so it felt as though I'd never left Texas.

I hadn't spent much of my profit from pot farming and still had well over two hundred and fifty thousand dollars in cash stuffed in my canvas tote bag—in the marijuana trade you deal strictly in cash. I took a serious look at my life and decided I should start thinking about my old age and figured I'd better not keep all my eggs in one basket. So, using my father's name and address—actually it was my name also, I answered to "Junior" until I joined the navy—I deposited two hundred thousand in a six-month CD to be rolled over until I closed the account. Interest from the CD would be deposited in a pass book account out of which rent for my safe-deposit box would be automatically deducted.

For the next couple of months I went over to Juarez three or four times a week and bought as many fifty peso gold pieces as I could stuff into my boots and still walk. I had nearly five hundred coins by the end of the second month (except for recognizable collectibles it was illegal for Americans to own gold between 1934 and 1971; President

Richard Nixon ended the restriction when he suspended the Bretton Woods Agreement). Owning gold had several advantages. Except for rare coins, it couldn't be traced. You could exchange it for paper currency almost anyplace in the world. And—according to my father who lived through the Great Depression—unlike paper money, gold would always hold its value. Also according to my father, it didn't rot when buried in the ground. The rest of the money, except for a couple of thousand dollars, I stashed away in my safe-deposit box.

My plans were to keep a low profile, scout out some remote area with enough water to grow marijuana and after a year or so go back into business. I rented an old rundown adobe on the outskirts of town, bought a used pickup truck and ordered a couple dozen topographical maps of federal lands in Texas and New Mexico. While waiting for the maps to arrive I drove up to the Panhandle about three o'clock one morning, and making sure no one saw me, not even my parents, buried the coins on my father's ranch. If the DEA came around asking questions, I didn't want my parents to know of my whereabouts. My planning was all for naught.

I hired a young señorita from down the street to cook, do my laundry, and take care of the house; pretty soon she was taking care of a lot more than the house. When her mother stopped by to find out why Juanita was spending so much time cleaning my house and found her daughter naked and in bed performing services not usually considered housekeeping duties, she, like any good Catholic, crossed herself, uttered a short prayer, and while clutching at her rosary ran from the house still praying. Juanita grabbed her clothes and ran after her mother. Before I knew it Juanita's father showed up with the sheriff and I was hauled off to jail and charged with statutory rape.

The case never went to court. The judge, being perhaps somewhat lenient on a fellow Texan, had the sheriff bring me into his chambers where he gave me a choice of ten years in jail or getting out and staying out of Texas and specifically El Paso. I didn't have any problem making a decision with the given options; however, there was a fly in the ointment. The judge, to make sure I got out of Texas and stayed out, had an army recruiter and the military police from nearby Fort Bliss standing by. The judge volunteered me for military service and since the army wasn't too particular about who they recruited as long as they were willing to go to Viet Nam, I was inducted into the army on the spot.

As fate would have it, after three month's training at Fort Benning, Georgia, I was transferred to, of all places, Fort Lewis in Washington

State, a mere 100 miles from the area where I had worked as a choker setter and hook tender for the timber industry, engaged in the lucrative business of pot farming, and where I had shot and killed a federal agent only six months earlier. Well, it didn't make much difference now—what could be worse, facing a murder warrant or a court martial for desertion? I hoped I would never find out.

I was deep in thought and failed to see Candi enter the diner and didn't notice her until she slipped into the booth beside me, placed her hand on my inner thigh, and gave a little squeeze.

"Everything okay?"

"It is now."

Wasted Opportunities

My first liberty in the Philippine Islands wasn't just a milestone in my race toward manhood; it was my introduction to the ways of the world and if for no other reason will remain at the top of my all-time list of things to remember. However, from a scholastic standpoint, Olongapo was grammar school whereas Candi was a college education.

I don't know what time I awoke, nor did I care, but at the very moment I stirred and opened my eyes Candi placed a tray with hot coffee and cinnamon rolls on the bedside table and came back to bed. Much to my delight, recess was over. Between classes we talked and Candi chronicled her life, and it was hard to tell whether or not she was proud of things she'd done or regretted the road she had taken. Her mood swings, as she moved from one segment of her life to another, led me to believe there was a little of both. However, it was easy, although painful, to look back at wasted opportunities. We were not eager to admit it, but we both knew our downhill slide had begun the day we left home, to what end we didn't know—only time would tell.

Candi had grown up in La Jolla, a coastal area of greater San Diego. La Jolla was at the opposite end of the social and economic scale from National City, where I had lived with my Filipino wife. Candi lived the life most little girls only fantasize about and was the daughter of every mother's dream. She studied drama, was a cheerleader, played piano, took ballet, and was a straight-A student. The year I was discharged from the navy she was just finishing her first year of high school. During summer vacation she began hanging out with the surfers at Mission Beach. A month later she had her own board and was "hot-dogging" with the best of them. Surfing wasn't the only thing Candi was attracted to at Mission Beach. The rhetoric served up by the antiestablishment made her feel guilty for the advantages she enjoyed due to the success of her parents. Beguiled by the New Left ideology, she became enamored with the new Bohemian's lifestyle. Soon she was wearing bright-colored skirts and peasant blouses, bells on her ankles, flowers in her hair, and painted pictures on her face. As a member of the new order of Gypsies, she had a conscience free of all responsibility for her parents' success and blameless for past luxuries.

Candi began her sophomore year a different person with a new look and a new language. Soon her friends were avoiding her and she was constantly at odds with her parents. Before long she started cutting classes and spending more time at the beach. Eventually, she dropped out of school, left home, and moved in with a group of new friends crowded into a small apartment in Pacific Beach. But the day of the flower child was short-lived. As the more militant hippies began to dominate the subculture, marijuana and various hallucinatory drugs were made available to pretty young runaway girls who needed extra courage to keep from returning home and begging their parents' forgiveness. Sex guaranteed she would have a place to stay, food to eat, and, of course, more drugs.

As her life continued to deteriorate and heavier drugs came into play she drifted up the coast in search of the real action. Like gold, the good times were always further on. You just missed it, you should have been here last year, or last month—the hippies' mantra as they described the good times. Candi continued her search in San Francisco, then Seattle, and finally Juneau, Alaska, and began to wonder if there had ever been any good times for anyone in the counterculture movement. The only good times she remembered were days spent with her parents and going to school with her friends while growing up in La Jolla. One thing she knew for sure—if she continued on the path she was traveling she would die without ever seeing her twenty-fifth birthday. Unlike those around her who were trying to justify their lifestyle by predicting an early death for themselves as part of the price of what they called freedom, she did not want to die young. She walked into a hospital emergency room, told them she was an addict and asked for help. She was turned over to social services, who put her on a methadone program which did nothing more than allow her to exchange one dependency for another, but even so, she kept sliding back to her old ways until in the end she decided to go cold turkey. She'd heard talk of people going cold turkey, but didn't know anyone who'd gone through the agonies of withdrawal successfully. But she had reached the point where it seemed her only hope.

With her last state subsistence check Candi bought a couple dozen packages of Twinkies, a bag of oranges, a bag of apples, a bottle of sleeping pills and a case of Baileys. She spent the rest of the money to pay two weeks in advance for a room at the Summit in Juneau. After locking the deadbolt on the door she wrapped the key in tissue paper and flushed it down the toilet, figuring if she stayed drunk enough and sleepy enough while eating just enough to stay alive and with no key to the door she wouldn't be able to get out of the room and score.

It was almost three weeks later when the hotel manager found her. When they checked her into the hospital she was weak and dehydrated, but alive and she wasn't thinking about a fix; she knew she had kicked the habit. Candi also knew, with no way to support herself, she would be tempted and might fall back into the lifestyle she had managed to escape by going cold turkey, so she gave the doctor her parents' names and telephone number. It wasn't surprising she remembered the phone number—she had thought about calling many times, and once when she actually called and her father answered she couldn't find the courage to speak. All she could do was cry and hang up the phone.

Her parents arrived the next day and stayed until the doctor released her, then took her back to La Jolla. Candi thought she could take up her old life where she'd left off, but things had changed. Her high school friends had all left home and were either in college or pursuing careers. Although her parents tried to be helpful and never asked questions, she knew they weren't stupid and had a pretty good idea of how she'd lived and the things she'd done to survive, but could only guess at the extent of her involvement. She knew they were wondering if and when she would come home with a buzz on or not come home at all. She couldn't stay, too much had changed, so she packed a bag with all the new clothes her parents had bought her, took some of her mother's jewelry and what money she could find, left a note explaining her dilemma and once again disappeared.

Candi was fortunate inasmuch as she decided to hold on to the jewelry for the proverbial rainy day; her rainy day was just around the corner. She used the money for a ticket to Denver and after taking a six-month lease on a nice apartment she still had enough left over to live comfortably for several months. Determined to support herself and not end up back in the trap she'd managed to escape she began seeking employment, but found being a high school dropout with no work history a severe handicap. Candi took a job as a cocktail waitress, but soon found working and supporting herself wasn't as romantic as it sounded and started looking for easier ways to make money. She met and married a guy with the same political convictions and economic philosophy, but her marriage was short-lived. It ended while she sat behind the wheel of a stolen car waiting for her husband to rob a convenience store. The owner of the store chose to shoot the guy rather than give him any money. Candi drove away while her husband lay bleeding to death on the sidewalk. She ditched the car, stuffed a few things in a backpack and headed west.

Candi knew she was getting ripped off when she sold her mother's jewelry, but when selling stolen jewelry you are in no position to haggle and you take whatever you can get; even at ten cents on the dollar she had more than seven thousand dollars when she reached Seattle. As disgusting as the thought of working and becoming a part of the capitalist system may have been to Candi, she truly intended to get a job and use the money to go back to school and make a decent life for herself. But again, planning was easier than doing and within a year her money was gone. Not wanting to end up answering questions about her husband's death and having to explain her part in the attempted robbery, she altered the names on her marriage certificate before applying for welfare, claiming her husband had abandoned her. Living on welfare forced her out of a comfortable apartment into a rundown trailer and the reality of having flushed her life down the toilet hit home when she entered her first topless dance contest.

There was no smile on her lips or sparkle in her eyes when she said, "I had spent all day taking a long hard look at myself and the life I was destined for; I had even contemplated ending it all, but couldn't bring myself to suicide. As I climbed onto the stage last night I was thinking I would sell my soul to the devil if he would erase the last ten years of my life and allow me to start high school again. But I figured Satan wasn't making any deals until the spotlights came on and I looked down into the dark piercing eyes of the devil himself. He was wearing Levis and cowboy boots, but he was the devil, right enough, and why wouldn't he be—hadn't I just agreed to sell him my soul if he would give me back my life? Well, if he was the devil I was determined to make good on my promise if he would deliver me from the misery and heartbreak I went to bed with every night and woke up to every morning."

When she looked at me the smile was playing across her lips again and the sparkle was back in her eyes. She put her face next to mine and asked, "D. B. Cooper, are you really the devil?"

"Some people seem to think so," I answered.

"What kind of life are you going to buy me? You promised to buy me a new life."

"Well then there now. You didn't wait very long to get back around to that."

"Well, I made good on my promise, didn't I?" Before I could answer, she asked, "Were you lying just to take advantage of me or do you intend to make good on your promise?"

"Look lady, if that's what you think I can pay you for your services and be on my way. I'm sure it won't be the first time you've slept with someone for money."

"That was a mean thing to say." For a moment I thought she was going to cry.

"Well, you weren't all that tactful yourself. You practically accused me of lying."

"I'm sorry, but in the past ten years I haven't run into many men who didn't take advantage of me, one way or another."

"Welcome to the club. Every woman I've met since I left home was only concerned with what was in it for her, but that didn't keep me from trusting you."

"Okay, I'm sorry, but I'm going to continue asking. You're my last chance. I'm willing to do whatever it takes as long as it's a two-way street."

"Well, it looks like we both made a lot of mistakes we wouldn't repeat if, knowing what we know today, we could have do-overs. But we know that's not going to happen, don't we?"

"I know, but I just want to get back everything I've lost. I keep hoping someone will come along and wave a magic wand and the past ten years will have never happened."

"Well, first of all, neither one of us lost anything—we threw it away. And second, you can't get back time. Once it's past, it's history. But that's not to say we can't make up for the time we threw away and perhaps even jump ahead."

"How?"

"Well, you said you were willing to do anything if it would get you a new life. Did you really mean it or was that just talk?"

"I meant it."

"Are you a gambler?"

"I took a chance on you—that was a gamble and I still don't know if I'm a winner or a loser."

"Are you willing to gamble the rest of the life you have now against a chance for a really good life? In other words, are you willing to go to prison if we fail?"

"What could happen to me in prison that hasn't already happened? I mean, how bad could it be? You don't have to work or worry about your next meal or whether or not you'll have a place to sleep. They provide clothes, medical care and I hear they even have color television. So, what do you have in mind?"

"I didn't say I had anything in mind—all I'm saying is, there are ways to make a lot of money in a hurry if you're willing to gamble, and when you gamble there's always the chance of losing."

"So, don't get caught."

"Nobody ever plans on getting caught, but no matter how well you plan, the unexpected can always happen and land you in jail. But hey, let's not talk about it right now, come over here and convince me you are really worth my taking a chance on going to prison."

"Oh, I'm worth it all right and you know it."

"Yeah, well, I've got a short memory and I'm going to need a lot of reminding, okay?"

"Oh, I'll remind you, I'll remind you in ways you'll never forget. I'll be the first thing you think about when you wake in the mornings and I'll be the last thing on your mind before you go to sleep, and when you dream, you'll dream about me."

Something New and Different

In referring to prison, Candi wasn't all that far wrong when she asked, "How bad can it be?" She lived in an old run-down trailer park, as coincidence would have it, just north of McCord Air Force Base and directly in the flight path of their main runway. When an aircraft took off you could barely think, much less hear anyone talk. None of the trailers had been moved in at least twenty years and would probably have fallen apart if anyone tried. Candi rented an old Spartan; the bed and tiny bathroom, opposite the only clothes closet, took up half the space while the other half served as the kitchen, dining, and living room. The entire trailer was only 8 feet wide and 25 feet long. The water heater didn't work—if you wanted a hot bath you had to get to the community shower early and even then it was only lukewarm. There was no air conditioning, the furnace hadn't worked in years, and the only source of heat was a portable electric heater. Candi had come a long way from La Jolla and it had all been downhill. She was only one step away from living out of a locker in the bus station. Speaking from experience, except for the freedom to go and come as you please, I can honestly say that for her prison might have been a step up.

As for me, I'd had my time in prison and didn't want a second installment, but I was willing to take a chance on doing the time if I could come up with something I thought had a 95 percent chance of succeeding—nothing is a 100 percent. If you start out thinking you have a perfect plan you are already in trouble; however, there was one thing I considered even more important than the odds of success or failure. The encounter with the DEA agent had made me realize that when a gun is used in a crime, somebody can end up dead, which means, if you're caught, a very long prison term and possibly the death penalty. Another consideration—the person ending up dead is oftentimes the guy with the gun. After the incident in my marijuana patch I decided never to use a gun when engaged in any type of illegal activity. Doing the crime is dumb enough, but using a gun while committing a crime is double dumb. Okay, so I'm pretty dumb and I will probably remain that way, otherwise I would have already changed my ways, but you'll never catch me double dumb.

I had come up with a few ideas on how to get my hands on some big bucks, but anything with potential required taking too many chances; what I needed was something new and different, something no one had tried before. The more I thought about it the more I realized I was onto something. The authorities would not have a ready plan of action, it would take time to organize and decide how to proceed. Every second the authorities delayed increased the chances for success. The more I thought about it the better I liked it, but there was a problem. Everything I considered had already been tried, one way or another and most had been unsuccessful.

The money I extorted from the credit card companies on the night I deserted the army hadn't lasted very long and to make ends meet Candi and I worked the badger game on unsuspecting GIs, until she set up a Special Forces guy who kicked my butt to the point I thought he was going to kill me. While recuperating, I decided to take a chance on getting the money I had stashed in the safe-deposit box in El Paso. I had been thinking about trying to get it for some time, but I was afraid the army had contacted the bank and if I showed up somebody at the bank would call and alert the authorities to the fact that I was still alive and had indeed deserted.

I had been checking the newspapers and watching the local news for any mention of my name in connection with either desertion or suspected foul play, but nothing had appeared. However, there was an article I found very interesting and although I couldn't explain why, I kept thinking about it. According to the story a soldier stationed in South Viet Nam by the name of George Hardin had tried to commandeer an Air Force C-141. He walked on board the aircraft, pointed an M-16 at some of the crew members and told them he wanted to go to Da Nang. When he suspected the crew was using delaying tactics he shot the loadmaster just to prove he was serious. He almost succeeded. He forced the crew to fire up the engines and taxi into takeoff position, and the only thing that kept the plane from taking off was the base commander's decision to block the runway. Eventually, the would-be hijacker got careless and the crew jumped him and took away the M-16. According to the article, Hardin remained calm during the entire incident, which lasted about forty-five minutes. He remained cool and collected even after being overpowered and while being held down, he calmly asked, "Aren't you guys going to let me up?"

When told no, he still did not panic and said, "Then there's a good chance that grenade in my pocket will go off."

As it turned out, there was no grenade, Hardin was bluffing, but according to one of the people involved, the thought of getting blown up sure had everyone's attention.

I wondered what Hardin was thinking. He had to have known, even if he'd gotten airborne, the authorities would be waiting for him when he landed. I would've written it off to just another dumb act, except for the fact that the guy was so calm. My guess was he had something in mind other than going to Da Nang, but what? Oh well, I had other things to think about, mainly, how to get to El Paso.

When I told Candi about the money in El Paso she was excited and said, "Let's go get it."

Then she asked, "How much is there?"

"Enough for us to get by on for a while." I answered.

She wasn't exactly happy with my answer and snapped, "I'm tired of just getting by—how much is there?" There was an ugly side to Candi and even though she had me under her spell, I had my doubts about her and had already decided it would behoove me not to trust her 100 percent. However, I couldn't think of a reason not to tell her how much money was in the bank box, providing it was still there—there was always the chance the Feds had found it and confiscated it. As though reading my mind, she asked sarcastically, "What's wrong, don't you trust me?"

"Look lady, don't get your panties in a wad. Like I said, there's enough for us to live on until we figure out a way to get our hands on some big bucks. There's somewhere around twenty-five or thirty thousand dollars, maybe a little more." Candi's eyes got real big, that devilish little smile of hers crept across her face and she whispered the question, "Thirty thousand dollars?"

"Yeah, I'm not sure exactly, but it's in the neighborhood of thirty grand, give or take a few thousand."

She repeated the amount several times; her attitude changed and she became once again the Candi I delighted in as she reached out her hand and said, "Come over here, D. B. Cooper, and tell me how you came by all that money."

Oh yeah, she was a witch all right, but what the hell?

Candi picked up her subsistence check and paid two months' rent for the trailer, which left us with less than thirty dollars except for the two hundred bucks I had stashed in my boot. I hadn't told Candi about the two hundred dollars yet—I'd been holding it back in case of an emergency. I had considered using the money for bus fare, but I didn't want to be flat broke when I got to El Paso. The idea didn't go over well with Candi; she had a hissy when I suggested going alone. She said I was just looking for a chance to leave her and once I got the money I wouldn't come back. She may have been right.

The night I told Candi my name was D. B. Cooper and I had deserted from the army I knew I would eventually need identification. If for no other reason, I wanted to have a driver's license in case I was stopped by the police. I remembered a sailor from Wyoming I used to bike with back in San Diego. Unfortunately for him, but fortunately for me, he took a spill on Highway 94 out near Barrett Junction and killed himself. Since we'd both grown up on ranches we had quite a bit in common and became pretty good friends. I remembered enough about him to satisfy the authorities in Cheyenne and was able to obtain a copy of his birth certificate. I then took the birth certificate to the social security office and told them I'd lost my social security number and didn't remember it. About a month later a social security card showed up in Candi's mailbox. With two pieces of identification it was easy to get a driver's license.

I hadn't given up my denims and cowboy boots, but by now I had shoulder-length hair and a full beard which matched up well with Candi's flower-child look. The summer of love had come and gone, Woodstock was history, and the hippies' days were numbered—time changes everything—but there were still a lot of hangers-on along Highway 101 and it was pretty easy hitchhiking to San Francisco. We spent four dollars and fifty cents at Goodwill for a dress, a pair of shoes and a handbag for Candi. I spent another four bucks for a shave and a haircut. When we walked into the Auto-Drive-Away office we looked, from the establishment viewpoint, fairly presentable. The man I'd talked with on the phone seemed relieved when he saw us—I can only imagine what he expected. A driver's license was all I needed to get a drive-away car destined for Dallas. A lot of people don't like driving across country, so they pay a company to deliver their car to wherever they're going; the company then finds a driver willing to deliver the car at his own expense. This works well for everyone concerned—the owner gets his car delivered, the company makes money, and the driver has transportation to his destination.

The Auto-Drive-Away company gave us a week to deliver a 1969 Pontiac Bonneville to Dallas. I didn't want to take any chances on getting stopped by the Highway Patrol, so I drove the speed limit all the way. Three days later I eased the Pontiac into a motel parking lot on the east end of El Paso. As things turned out, I couldn't have planned it better had I tried. We arrived on Thursday, the twenty-eighth of August and as luck would have it, Labor Day was the first of September. Labor day is always a long weekend and being the last holiday of summer it meant just about everybody had plans and was eager to get a head start, especially those with travel plans. It was my guess no one at the bank would want to start a line of questioning that might delay the beginning of their long weekend.

After paying for a room for the night we still had almost a hundred and forty dollars left from my holdout stash. We cleaned up and rested for a couple of hours before driving into *Old Town* to La Paloma Blanca—a cantina I remembered from the few months I'd lived in El Paso—where I tried to make up for all the Tex-Mex cooking I'd missed since leaving home. After dinner I located the bank and cruised around a bit refamiliarizing myself with the streets and making sure I knew the quickest way out of El Paso. I also memorized a second way out of town just in case there were some last-minute surprises along my intended route.

Back at the motel I used my knife to pry the heel off my boot. The key to the bank box along with the receipt, wrapped in Saran wrap, looked just the same as they did the day I put them in the hollowed-out boot heel. I mixed the contents of two tubes of epoxy I'd purchased from an auto parts store and glued the heel back in place.

We slept late the next day. At nine thirty I called the bank to double-check on the hours they would be open. I didn't want to take a chance the bank would give their employees a jump on the long weekend by closing early. We checked out of the motel just before noon. I was hoping a guy would be in charge of checking identification for anyone wanting to get into their lockbox and figured Candi would be a good distraction, but she needed to dress the part. At the El Paso Saddle and Blanket Company I located their used-clothing section and bought her a pair of boots, some tight-fitting jeans, an equally tight-fitting western-style shirt, and a well-worn Stetson. She made a few snide remarks about her new outfit, but I think she liked it; I thought she looked sexier than I had ever seen her. I'd done everything I could think of to provide us with the best chance of getting into the box, getting the money, and getting out of town without having anyone suspect the Feds might be interested in me.

After filling the Pontiac's gas tank I cruised past the bank and drove my intended route out of town one last time before heading back to La Paloma Blanca for some more Tex-Mex. When we finished eating I went to the restroom and took one last prop from under the insole of my boot and slipped it into my wallet. Once I started thinking about getting into the bank box I knew I would need at least one piece of identification, so I used a trick I had learned in Vacaville. Before we left Tacoma I had used the copy machine at the post office to make a copy of my old navy buddy's birth certificate. At the library I used whiteout to cover his name, date, and place of birth, then used one of their typewriters to put my real name, date, and place of birth over the whiteout. Back at the post office I made a copy of the altered birth certificate; the whiteout was undetectable. I did the same thing with the social security card, and then used the two altered documents to get a driver's license in my real name. I still didn't want Candi to know my real name so I hid the driver's license in my boot and destroyed the altered documents—Candi was unaware I hid things in my boots.

At two forty, just twenty minutes before closing time, we walked into the bank; nothing inside had changed, everything was just as I remembered. As I approached the counter I realized a woman, not a man as I'd hoped, was at the teller's cage where they passed you through into the vault, so I directed Candi to one of the couches in the waiting area and told her to fake reading a magazine while keeping an eye on the lady after she let me into the vault to see if she appeared excited and talked to anyone or made any phone calls. She opened her mouth to ask a question or most likely protest. I know she wanted to make sure I didn't try anything tricky with the money, but thought better of it and did just as I asked.

I figured if I engaged the woman in conversation it would distract her and she might overlook a note, if there was one, attached to my signature card, so I approached the counter and said, "Howdy, how you doing?"

She was about my own age, maybe a couple of years younger and a little on the plump side, but fairly pretty.

"I'm fine, thank you."

She was pleasant enough and polite, but her voice was melancholy and her question, "How can I help you?" lacked enthusiasm.

I didn't know if she had problems or just didn't want to be there—either way, I figured I'd better keep talking. I handed her my key and receipt to the bank box and said, "I need to get into my safe-deposit box for a couple of minutes."

I then asked, "Got a big weekend planned?" She placed a signature card in front of me and while looking through her files for my original signature card said, "Not unless you consider staying home and cleaning house a big weekend."

I signed the card, pushed it across to her side of the counter and said, "That doesn't sound like a lot of fun; maybe we should get together and do a little (Texas) two-stepping this weekend." She asked for a piece of identification and when I handed over the fake driver's license she compared the signature on the driver's license to the signature I'd just scribbled on the card, then compared them both to the original. After placing the original signature card in the file drawer she handed the fake driver's license back to me, dropped the card I'd just signed into a second drawer, and then glanced over at Candi and asked, "What would your girlfriend have to say about that?"

"Nothing." I waited a couple of seconds, and then continued, "She'd probably fill my backside full of buckshot, but she wouldn't say anything."

That brought a smile to her face. She pushed the buzzer and as I passed through the gate to her side of the counter she took another quick look at Candi and said, "I'll bet she would, she looks the type."

The lady used my key and one from a ring of keys she removed from a desk drawer to open the door and gain access to my box. She handed me the box and directed me to one of three small rooms.

"Call me when you're finished."

I figured since my gift of gab had gotten me this far there was no reason to abandon it now and commented, "How can I call you, I don't know your name, let alone your telephone number."

She smiled again, "My name is Maria."

"What about the phone number?"

"We'll talk about that the next time you stop by."

"Hey, it might be sooner than you think."

"You'd better check whatever you need to check in your box. We close in less than fifteen minutes."

"Yeah, right, thanks." I entered the little room and closed the door behind me, placed the box on the table and opened the lid. The paper bag was still there just as I'd left it. I carefully removed the bag, unfolded the top, and nervously looked inside. There was no need to count it, I knew no one had been inside the box. I'd forgotten the exact amount anyway. I refolded the bag, closed the box lid, opened the door, and was about to call to Maria when I remembered the driver's license I'd just used to gain access to the box. I wasn't about to take a chance Candi might get her hands on it. In the beginning I hadn't told Candi the truth about who I was and what I had done because I didn't want to take the chance she might let it slip accidentally, but now I was convinced, and I couldn't explain why, if she figured she could get a big reward for turning me in to the authorities she wouldn't think twice and I'd be doing time in Leavenworth. I knew I could never fully trust her and in the end she would be my undoing and I would be better off dumping her the first chance I got. But I knew I would never leave her, witch or not—I was under her spell. I opened the box again and dropped the driver's license inside and then called to Maria. I waited while she replaced the box in the appropriate slot and locked the little door. When she handed me my key I said, "I don't have enough time to look through all this stuff and find the information I need before you close, so I'll just take everything home, find what I need and bring it back next week." Maria pushed a button which sounded a buzzer and opened the gate to the lobby. I passed through the gate, then turned back and gave her a sheepish grin, before adding, "Maybe you'll give me your telephone number when I come back."

She smiled, pulled the hair back from the right side of her face and replied, "Maybe."

Candi looked like she'd been sitting on a cactus the way she jumped up from the couch and hurried toward me. I had my back to Maria and no one at the counter could see me when I put my hand up, signaling her to slow down, then as she was about to speak, I moved my finger to my lips. She got the message and we strolled out of the bank and around the corner to the car without talking. When we were inside the car I tossed the bag onto her lap and said, "That should get us by for a while."

When she looked inside her eyes got as big as saucers and I'd never seen them so bright. I headed due north out of El Paso on Highway 54, still sticking to the speed limit. A couple of hours later we passed through Alamogordo, and ten minutes later I turned onto Highway

70 toward Roswell. Another three hours put us exactly where I wanted to be, the Texas Panhandle. If anything went wrong I wanted to be on familiar ground. But nothing went wrong, everything went down as smooth as ExLax. We delivered the Bonneville to Dallas as promised, then I looked through the advertisement section of the newspaper and after a half dozen telephone calls bought a 1964 pickup truck with a slide-in camper from a guy who had just been drafted into the army.

I was anxious to get out of Texas, so I headed north again through Oklahoma City and didn't turn west until we reached Kansas. Candi was already making plans on how to spend her newfound wealth; I put a stop to her planning real fast, telling her in no uncertain terms, we were not going to blow the money. She pouted for a while, but after counting the money a couple of times and talking about all the things we would do when we got some really big bucks she became the playful Candi of old and before long I was having trouble concentrating on my driving.

By the end of November my hair and beard had grown out again and Candi was back to her flower-child look. However, she kept the clothes I'd bought her in El Paso. I don't know if it was because she liked them or because I told her they made her look sexy. I still hadn't come up with a plan. Something was forming in the back of my mind as bits and pieces played across my subconsciousness from time to time, but I just couldn't get it focused.

By the first of December the weather was getting pretty damp and chilly, so we paid four months' rent in advance, packed up the camper and headed for a warmer and drier climate. As we pulled out of the trailer park, a big Starlifter took off from McCord Air Force Base and climbed slowly until it disappeared into the gray skies of the Pacific Northwest. I figured it was on its way to Viet Nam and wondered if it was the one Hardin had tried to hijack. I still hadn't figured out what he intended to do with the airplane, I didn't believe he was just going to force the crew to take him to Da Nang as the article indicated because he had to know the authorities would be waiting for him when he landed. I figured he was either going to force the crew to land in North Viet Nam, thinking the Communists would compensate him for stealing and delivering the aircraft to them or he was planning to land in a country without an extradition treaty with the United States. Either way, I was betting he planned to defect and was hoping to end up with some money—probably he'd already made a deal and had been waiting for the right time to put his plan into action. It was obvious he hadn't put enough planning into his scheme and he certainly didn't pick the right time. I wondered what the Communists would pay for a C-141. As though reading my thoughts Candi asked, "How much do you think that airplane cost?"

"More than you and I could ever spend."

"I don't know, I could spend a lot."

She watched the big cargo plane until it disappeared, and then asked, "Wouldn't it be great to have enough money to escape all this materialism and go live in some exotic land?"

I guess I'll never know if Candi really didn't have a clue or was just whacked; she hated the rich, claimed to be a socialist and continually bad-mouthed capitalism while at the same time wishing for enough money to live in luxury. She didn't seem to understand if you wanted something you had to earn it through work and sacrifice or more likely, she didn't want to work and justified her misery by blaming the rich. To her anybody with more money than she had was rich, which was just about everyone. I wasn't all that interested in working for a living myself, at least not honest sweat-of-the-brow work. I preferred to find easier ways to make money, but I knew capitalism beat socialism any day of the week. My father's success was a testament to what a determined individual can accomplish through hard work and sacrifice in a capitalist society. Orphaned at sixteen he'd begun work as a ranch hand, he married my mother at twenty and they lived with her parents until he bought a small ranch at age twenty-four. At thirty-five he owned four sections and now—well I really don't know, last I knew he owned sixteen sections.

We spent the next three months in out-of-the-way parks along the coast, mostly in southern California. I headed down I-5 before cutting over to the coast at Eugene. We spent our first night at the Oregon Dunes, pretty much deserted except for a few dune buggy enthusiasts. The next morning Candi spread a blanket between a couple of dunes, stripped off her clothes, smeared baby oil all over her body and baked herself in the sun for most of the day. When I warned her against sunburn she said, "I don't burn."

She was right; she didn't even turn pink, let alone red, and after a couple of weeks was sporting an all-over honey brown tan. The weather in Oregon and northern California wasn't much warmer than in Tacoma so we didn't spend much time north of Morro Bay. Candi's love affair with the sun was rivaled only by her affection for the water. If she wasn't lying in the sun she was frolicking in the water. I had never seen her happier.

At Jalana Beach, an out-of-the-way park just north of Point Conception, Candi borrowed a surfboard from a couple of teenagers and within half an hour had a group of admirers oohing and aahing at her hot-dogging. It was obvious she hadn't lost her touch, even though many years had passed since she had learned to surf at Mission Beach in San Diego. We stopped in Santa Barbara and bought her a surfboard and a wet suit—the water temperature along the California coast in December is around sixty degrees. For the rest of the winter, except for a few days around Christmas, she was in heaven.

Candi's emotions ran the entire gamut. She could be as tender as a kitten or as tough as nails, a passionate lover one minute and icy cold the next. Her smiles and laughter turned to frowns and sarcasm without warning—she might be all a-twitter with eye-sparkling excitement and a moment later be withdrawn and depressed. Her mood swings were unpredictable, but in all the time I knew her I saw her cry only once. We were staying at San Onofre State Beach, where for a couple of dollars a night we could park the camper on Old Highway 101 between Interstate 5 and the cliffs overlooking the Pacific Ocean. From there it was an easy walk down to the beach. Candi loved San Onofre. She would walk north along the sand for about a mile to Trestle Beach where the surf was better, then after spending all day surfing, on the way back she used the showers at the Marine Corps Beach Recreation Center to wash off the salt and sand. Most of the beach between San Clemente and Oceanside belongs to Camp Pendleton, and San Onofre State Beach is surrounded by Camp Pendleton. Sometimes I went with her to Trestle Beach, but it being Sunday I decided to stay in the camper and watch football—the camper was equipped with a motor-generator which supplied power for the television and other accessories. It was midafternoon when Candi arrived back at the camper with a strange look about her and without an explanation asked if we could go to San Diego. When I questioned her she said she wanted me to see where she used to live. I doubted that was the reason and suspected she had seen someone she knew from her past. Whether or not she talked with them I didn't know, and I didn't ask. Whatever the case might have been, the encounter—and I'm only guessing she met or saw someone— stirred something inside her which served up a huge plate of melancholy and she wanted to take a look at what might have been. Since I had always been curious about where she grew up and wondered what kind of life she had thrown away, I agreed without trying to ascertain her true motive.

Weekend traffic returning to Los Angeles from San Diego, Tijuana, and Baja was backed up over 2 miles at the INS checkpoint on I-5 north of Oceanside, but we were unaffected as southbound traffic toward San Diego was light. Candi wanted to drive along the coast so we cut over to Highway 1 at Carlsbad and drove through the beach towns. She kept up a running monologue, pointing out landmarks along the way. I hadn't told her nor did I intend to tell her about my tour in the navy or that I had lived in National City and was quite knowledgeable of San Diego County. I played dumb, expressed interest, asked questions, and pretended to be impressed.

Remembering Southern California's spectacular sunsets and noticing the sun was hanging just above the horizon like a giant red ball, I eased the camper off the road just below Del Mar where the highway parallels the ocean, almost at the water's edge, and we watched the sun slip into the Pacific. A few minutes later the sky lit up like a kaleidoscope of red and orange. We watched until the colors faded away and we began to lose the light before I pulled back onto the highway and started up Torrey Pines Grade. I noticed Candi had become pensive and suddenly silent. I suspected she was reliving episodes from her past, whether the recent or distant past I didn't know, and didn't ask. Considerable time passed before she broke her silence. There was no emotion in her voice when she said, "Turn right at Prospect."

It was the last weekend before Christmas and La Jolla was all decked out in her holiday dress. Stores played Christmas music and displayed animated fairy-tale scenes in their windows, shoppers were carrying packages wrapped in brightly colored paper, and everyone was in a festive mood. I remembered how exciting Christmas was when I was a youngster growing up in Texas and was about to relate those memories to Candi, but thought better of it when I saw the doleful expression on her face. I can't remember having seen anyone or anything looking as sad as Candi looked at that moment.

"Turn right just past the La Valencia, then left on Coast Boulevard."

The words were barely audible. She continued to direct me along narrow streets and several sharp turns. I had the feeling she wasn't taking any particular route and only wanted to take one last look at her old neighborhood. I remembered Candi telling me the house she grew up in was built on a hillside and had seven terraced levels with stairs down to the beach. I drove slowly, expecting her to point out her parents' home, but she didn't. However, somewhere in the vicinity of Bird Rock her head turned slowly to the right and she continued to look back until the road curved uphill away from the water. When she turned around I could see tears streaming down her face. She quickly turned away and said, "Get the hell out of here."

I felt sorry for her, but it had been her doing, not mine. I could empathize with Candi. There were times I regretted having ever left Texas, but empathy wasn't going to fix anything for either of us, so I did as she asked and headed for Interstate 5. When I reached the freeway I turned south, figuring the warm sands of Baja would cheer her up.

It was late February before we passed through the Tijuana-San Ysidro border crossing and headed north. Even though Candi had spent the better part of the winter surfing, she wanted to catch a few last waves at Trestle beach before going back to Tacoma. The marines were engaged in some sort of exercise moving troops and equipment from ships offshore to the beach by way of landing craft and helicopters. Supposedly, some rogue nation had overrun a small country allied with the United States and it was the marines' job to expel the invaders. On the third day the level of activity increased considerably. The marines were using hovercraft to establish a beachhead, and jet fighters capable of landing, taking off, and hovering almost like helicopters patrolled the skies and occasionally fired missiles at targets in the cliffs above the beach. It was all very interesting and I decided to stay up on the cliffs and watch for a while, figuring I would join Candi at Trestle Beach after lunch.

I wasn't alone. Several other campers had the same idea and set up all sorts of things including chairs, tables with umbrellas, and telescopes on tripods, and some brought ice chests full of food and drinks. I hadn't been on the cliffs long when someone pointed toward a half dozen C-130 transports heading toward the coast. Lately, anytime I saw a military cargo plane I thought about George Hardin and his attempt to hijack a Starlifter. I just couldn't get the incident out of my mind. Shortly after the aircraft crossed the beach, paratroopers started jumping from the rear of the airplanes and in less than a minute the sky was filled with olive-drab-colored canopies. Three waves of C-130s flew over with each plane expelling paratroopers from its rear cargo hatch. It was exciting to watch, but after a couple of hours the sun was beginning to cook my brain so I headed back to the camper for something cold to drink. I popped the top on one of the Dos Equs I'd brought back from Mexico and for no particular reason started thinking about Hardin again, and then it hit me like a ton of bricks. I knew how I was going steal a million dollars and how I was going to escape. All I had to do was work out the details. It would require a lot of planning to make it work, but it was a stroke of genius, a new and different crime guaranteed to make every headline in the country and probably the world. It was so simple I couldn't believe it hadn't been tried already. Well, no doubt there would be many copycats, but being first I would have the best chance of success. The more I thought about it the more I believed it was as near perfect a crime as one could hope for with a 99 percent chance of succeeding.

I threw some sandwiches together, then dropped some ice cubes into a thermos jug and emptied a couple of 7ups along with a bottle of Gallo Chablis into the thermos to create Candi's drink of choice—she drank wine coolers by the gallon—grabbed a bag of chips and some paper cups, stuck it all inside a day pack and headed for Trestle Beach.

Candi was sitting on her board a hundred yards offshore, with a dozen other surfers, watching the next set approach. I spotted her bag, dropped my day pack onto her towel and sat down on the sand. It turned out to be a weak set and only a couple of surfers even tried for a takeoff. The next set was smoking and almost everybody caught the first wave. Candi passed on the first two, then caught the third wave with a clean takeoff and started hot-dogging along the face of the wave just in front of the curl. She spotted me and rode the wave almost to shore, walking her board to get as much out of the wave as she could. She climbed out of the water, dropped her board onto the sand, then plopped down beside me, gathered up her hair and began twisting it to squeeze out the water.

I filled a paper cup with the mixture from the thermos and handed it to her along with a sandwich. She emptied the cup without stopping, passed it back to me for a refill, and began eating the sandwich. I was excited about finally coming up with a plan and was eager to break the news to Candi. I guess I must have been grinning like the cat that ate the canary because she took one look at me and asked, "What?"

Her eyes were sparkling and she had that devilish little smile on her lips. I just kept grinning and looking at her. She opened the collar on her wet suit and unzipped it down to her navel—she was naked underneath the wet suit—and repeated the question. "What?"

This time there was excitement in her voice. I waited for a few moments, then answered, "I've got it."

"Got what?"

"Got a plan, it hit me smack in the face about an hour ago. It's exactly what I've been looking for, something new and different, something never tried before. It's as close to perfect as we could hope for and I'm confident we can pull it off without getting caught. But it will take a lot of time and planning before we're ready." Candi's excitement was growing, as was mine.

"What's your plan?"

"I'm going to steal an airplane." Candi looked at me as though I had lost my mind. Her excitement had been short-lived. Now there was obvious disappointment in her voice when she said, "You're crazy."

"Maybe so, but I'm going to steal a commercial airliner just the same."

"Sure you are," she said sarcastically.

"What are you going to do with your airplane?"

"I'm going to sell it."

"Who would be stupid enough to buy a stolen airliner?"

"The people who own it."

"You're a big phony, D. B. Cooper. You're never going to get your hands on any real money."

"I'm serious, think about it. If you owned something worth ten million dollars wouldn't you pay a million dollars to get it back?"

She thought about it for several seconds, her eyes began to sparkle again and she said, "You are serious, aren't you?"

"Damn straight."

Candi was getting excited again. "Did you say a million dollars?"

"How much do you want?"

She beamed for a few seconds. "How about two million?"

"Why not?"

She could hardly contain herself, and without taking a breath began firing questions at me, all beginning with how, what, or when.

"Not now, I'll tell you all about it later."

Without hesitating she said, "Let's get started."

She jumped up and began gathering her things.

"Don't you want to surf anymore?"

"Surfing can wait, let's go back to the camper. I want to hear all about how you're going to steal me two million dollars."

Working out the Details

I laid it all out for Candi, how I came up with the idea, how I intended to pull it off, and what we were going to do afterwards. Her eyes were brighter than I had ever seen them. She continued to fire questions at me inquiring into every detail. I had never seen her so excited, "Two million dollars!"

She repeated the figure several times. "Do you know all the things we can do with two million dollars?" She continued without waiting for me to respond. "We can go anyplace in the world we want to go, have all the things we've ever wished for and do anything we want to do no matter when it strikes our fancy. When are you going to do it?"

"In about six months if all goes well."

"Six months!" Her voice went up about two octaves and several decibels, as though she didn't believe what she was hearing.

"Why not next week?"

"Because we need at least six months for planning. What might seem like an insufficient detail, at the moment, could mean the difference between success and failure. The reason most people get caught is that they get an idea about some criminal endeavor and try putting it into action without thinking it through. Preparation is the key to success and I intend to be successful. I want to spend the money, not spend time in prison thinking about what went wrong. So if you want to help me spend those two million greenbacks you're going to have to commit to at least six months of research and planning."

"But six months seems like such a long time! Do you really need six months?"

"Look at me and listen to me very carefully. It's six months or not at all. If you have a better offer I suggest you take it, otherwise it's six months. It's up to you, so decide now or forget it."

"Okay, okay, six months." Irritation betrayed her disappointment at having to wait six months for "her money," otherwise her voice had returned to normal. Now that I think about it, her normal voice, except on rare occasions, was a mixture of bitterness, envy, yearning, and lack of fulfillment with one usually dominating the others according to her mood.

"Six months will go faster than you think. As a matter of fact, six months may be cutting it a little close."

"I know you're right, but you made it sound so easy I didn't think it would require so much time to figure out how to steal an airplane."

"Figuring out how to steal an airplane isn't the problem. Getting away without being caught after we have the money is the problem."

Candi became very serious. She may have been thinking about the consequences of getting caught, but more likely she was considering the cost of failure from another point of view. She was probably looking at this as her last chance to regain the life of luxury she had thrown away. Her frame of mind was evident by her next statement and I knew she had committed 100 percent to making it work.

"Okay, I'll do whatever it takes. What do we do first?"

"We go back to Tacoma and make a list of all the things we need to know, another list of all the equipment we need and most important of all, a list of things that can go wrong."

"What can go wrong—why a list?"

"Anytime you engage in any illegal undertaking a hundred things can go wrong and if you can think of fifty you're a genius. But every time you add something to your can-go-wrong list you improve your chances of success."

The more I explained the consequences of being poorly prepared the more serious she became. She never mentioned the time frame again, nor did she ever question any of my decisions during the planning stages. She had plenty of suggestions, and many were helpful. She was always pleased when I agreed with her and incorporated one of her recommendations into the plan. However, she never insisted I change anything and followed my instructions down to the last detail.

"How long will it take to drive to Tacoma?"

"Two or three days if we take our time. By leaving in the morning we should be there by the weekend."

"Let's leave now and drive straight through." From that moment on Candi put her every waking moment into making the hijacking a success. In the end she put more time and effort into planning and research, especially research, than I did. I doubt I would have gone through with it without her.

Candi's enthusiasm was contagious. By the time we reached Bakersville we had already established the area in which I would jump. The most important part of the jump was to survive, to reach the ground alive and with all your body parts intact. The next most important thing was to be on familiar ground when you landed—getting as far away from the crime scene as possible wasn't always the best policy, especially if it meant being in unfamiliar surroundings. The survival part meant I had to do everything I could to stack the odds in my favor and hope for the best, but the familiar ground was an easy decision. Cowlitz County in southwest Washington, where I had worked as choker setter and hook tender for Weyerhaeuser and where I did my pot farming, was perfect. I knew the Lewis River Valley like the back of my hand. Once I was on the ground I knew lots of places to hide and it would be almost impossible to spot me from the air even if they figured out where I jumped. If I waited until winter, most logging operations would be shut down for the year and not many people would be in the area. With any luck at all I'd be on an airplane heading for Hawaii before anyone started looking for me. While the authorities were out tramping through the woods Candi and I would be in a hotel in Waikiki drinking champagne and counting our money.

Deciding on the Lewis River Valley automatically determined the route the airplane would have to fly, south from Seattle or north out of Portland. We figured Portland to Seattle would be best, it would give the Feds—we assumed it would come under federal jurisdiction—less time to organize. The next thing was to decide on the type of aircraft, the military C-130 or C-141 with the rear cargo hatch would be ideal, but I wasn't going to mess around with the military. Fate seemed to be smiling on us. As it turned out Boeing was building the perfect aircraft for what I had in mind less than 50 miles from Tacoma. I didn't realize just how perfect the 727 was until we started gathering information on it.

The '27 was the only commercial airliner in service with an aft stair for loading or unloading passengers. This feature alone made it the aircraft of choice for any would-be hijacker. It became even more attractive after I learned it would fly as slow as 80 to 100 knots.

Candi started hanging out at restaurants and bars around Renton frequented by Boeing employees and before long had a stack of technical drawings, flight test data, and a current list of airlines flying the 727—I never asked how she got the information, but take it from me, if Candi wanted something she had ways of getting it. Candi became an expert on the '27 as she researched everything from the time planning had begun in the midfifties through rollout in late '62 and its first flight the following February. She could tell you the date the first '27 was delivered, (October 29, 1963) and knew that more than eight hundred (as of March 1970) were already in service, mostly in the United States. When it came to planning and trying to account for the unexpected, Candi was on top of it. She ruled out United Airlines since their aircraft had been involved in half of the eight 727 crashes in the United States (a total of thirteen had crashed worldwide through '69).

I knew absolutely nothing about parachutes and until I hit upon the plan to hijack an airplane, hadn't even in my wildest dreams thought about or had any desire to jump out of an airplane, especially one not on fire or about to crash. It didn't take a genius to figure out that attempting what I had in mind without ever having jumped out of an airplane with a parachute would be next to suicide, so I used a name I figured nobody would remember and drove down to Aurora, Oregon where a fledgling sport jumping club got together on weekends at the Pacific Parachute center. Weekends were about the only time you could get enough guys together to pay for the plane, if you didn't want to foot the bill by yourself. I considered doing just that—pay for everything and get done in a month what would take three or four months to accomplish on weekends, but aside from the expense I didn't want to attract undue attention and have someone associate me with the crime of the decade.

I paid fifty dollars for my first jump, which included instructions, reading material, and the use of a parachute and harness. All jumps after that were ten dollars each. I was required to make the first five jumps with a "dope rope" (static line). Static line jumps are supposed to be easy. It goes something like this: you jump out of the plane, hit the end of the static line, the canopy opens and you float down to earth. Well, for me it wasn't that simple. To begin with, pushing myself out of a perfectly good airplane for the first time was one of the hardest things I'd ever done. On impact I sprained my ankle and to make matters worse I couldn't collapse my canopy and lost about a pound of skin when a gust of wind dragged me across the landing zone. If that wasn't enough to discourage a second jump, at the very moment I finally did get my canopy to collapse the wind changed and blew the whole parachute back on top of me. I got tangled in the shroud lines and wrapped up in the canopy and thought I was going to smother before I could get untangled and free myself from the canopy. I wasn't in any danger of suffocating, but I was scared nevertheless and it didn't make getting back in the plane for the second jump any easier. About the only thing that didn't go wrong on my first jump was that the canopy opened. I figured sports parachuting was kind of like bronc busting—if you are thrown off the first time, you get up, dust yourself off, screw your Stetson down a little tighter and climb back on. So I got up, grabbed another parachute, laced my boots up a little tighter, and climbed back on board the airplane.

The second weekend I made my last static-line jump and my first hop-and-pop on the same day. After three hop-and-pops I was ready for my first free fall at 3,500 feet. I had been looking forward to my first free fall because I knew this would be a vital part of getting away with the money. It wasn't much of a free fall—it was supposed to be a five-second delay, but I yanked the ripcord immediately after exiting the airplane. Eight jumps later I was ready to jump from 5,500 feet with a delayed opening of twenty seconds, but I was still doing hop-and-pops, I just couldn't make myself count off the seconds. You increase altitude and opening delay in increments, three at 3,500 feet with a five-second delay, then three more at 3,500 feet with a ten-second delay. After that you move up in increments of a 1000 feet and five-second delays and eventually are cleared for 7,500 feet with a thirty-second delay. I was afraid the jump-master might not let me continue, since his policy was to dismiss anyone who might get himself or another jumper hurt. I was fortunate to meet a guy who had over two hundred jumps—he was obviously fearless. I told him of my problem and he suggested we go up together, I would jump first and after I opened my canopy he would jump and I could observe him during free fall. He was beautiful to watch. He stabilized almost immediately upon exiting, and then started gliding in my direction. He sailed right past me, did a somersault, stabilized again, did a flat spin, then another somersault before opening his canopy. On my next jump I wasn't so quick on the ripcord and stabilized without much of a problem. As a matter of fact, after stabilizing I was so overcome by the sensation of freedom I forgot about the ground rushing toward me at 200 feet per second and almost didn't get my canopy opened in time. My next jump went okay and a month later I had overcome all my fears and problems and was into acrobatics.

For the first two months I used the club's parachutes. There was talk about the Stratocloud, a new type of parachute for sports jumpers, referred to as a wing. Experiments with the Stratocloud were ongoing, but it had yet to be approved for sale to the public, The Paracommander was still the standard, but having decided on a small canopy, I purchased a LOPO. The LOPO (Low Porosity) was a round 26-foot canopy made by the Security Parachute Company. I selected the LOPO for two reasons: faster rate of descent after opening, and size. A LOPO and NB-6 container made a complete rig small enough to qualify as carry-on luggage without attracting undue attention. Otherwise, since the Security LOPO panels sometimes ripped because they were cut and sewn under fluorescent lights—the reason LOPO panels ripped wasn't known at the time—I would have used a 28-foot government surplus canopy with a double L and tojo cut. But I figured if the canopy didn't rip during my practice jumps, it would hold up for the one jump that really counted—the jump that would catapult me into history books. It might even make me a legend in my own time.

After laying out almost a thousand dollars for all-new equipment I realized why sports parachuting wasn't very popular. Besides the cost of equipment you had to provide your own transportation to and from drop zones, pay for a place to stay if you wanted to jump both days, and for the weekend you could lay out as much as fifty or sixty dollars in jump fees. The camper had been a good investment and was the perfect vehicle for the average sport parachutist; it provided transportation to and from the drop zone as well as shelter, hot meals, and cold beer.

I was able to get in five to six jumps most weekends and figured I would be well prepared by the end of September, providing we had good weekend weather. I was hoping to make at least seventy-five jumps. I was shooting for 100 jumps, but I was willing to settle for anything over fifty. With fifty openings I surmised I'd have enough experience to survive a jump from 10,000 feet with air speed at or above 100 knots.

In order to jump the LOPO in an NB-6 container (the NB-6 and harness for the LOPO was the Navy's emergency rig) I had to find a rigger who would sew D-rings into the harness for a front reserve; otherwise it wouldn't be legal for sport jumping. The jumpmaster wasn't all that happy about the rig not having Capewells, but since he was in it for the money and it was legal with a front reserve, he let me use it. Your only means of disconnecting from your main parachute without Capewells is to cut it away. In an emergency, opening your reserve with the main chute deployed and still attached could result in additional problems. I would have preferred having the quick-disconnect feature during my training jumps, but when the training was over and it came time for the big event it wouldn't matter whether or not I had Capewells, since I would be jumping without a reserve parachute. I planned to use the D-rings for the reserve to attach a canvas pouch full of hundred-dollar bills to my harness.

By this time Candi was really into what she had dubbed Operation Quick Rich and turned her attention to airlines flying 727s on regular schedules from Portland to Seattle. I gave her a set of parameters to work with and made it explicitly clear they must all be met or she could forget about getting her greedy little hands on two million dollars. My plans required that the flight depart Portland after the workday ended on either a Friday or the day before a holiday, preferably a long weekend. It seemed to me people were always eager to get away from work on Fridays more than anytime other than the beginning of a long weekend, when they were extra eager to leave. I reasoned there would be more confusion between law enforcement and airline executives on a weekend, when less experienced people were in charge, and figured that amid the confusion, the airline, not wanting to take a chance on losing their airplane, would be quicker to cough up the money. I also insisted the date be close enough to winter solstice to insure it would be dark by the time I bailed out with the money and if at all possible I wanted the advantage of jumping during the dark of the moon. This would make it difficult for anyone to spot me during the time I was in the air.

Whatever fears I may have had early on about jumping out of an airplane were long gone when I opened my canopy for the fiftieth time—the minimum number of jumps I had set for myself before fully committing to my plan—and I was confident I could safely make the jump from 10,000 feet at 100 knots and reach the ground with my body intact. I was well aware of Murphy's Law—if something can go wrong it will go wrong when you least expect it and at the worse possible moment—but you can't worry about what might happen. All you can do is prepare as best you can. I had been fortunate in one way, if you consider near disaster inspiring, but inasmuch as the mishap helped me work through an unforeseen and unanticipated problem without panicking, I considered it a stroke of good luck. On my forty-second jump I experienced a *streamer*. Air wasn't getting inside my canopy and it was just streaming out above me. I could have used my reserve and probably should have, but I remained calm and while racing toward the ground at 200 feet per second, climbed up the shroud lines and shook the canopy loose just as I had been taught by my jumpmaster. The incident could have ended with devastating results, even with a reserve chute. Better men than I have packed it in after having a problem getting their canopy to open properly, but for me it served as a confidence builder. The opening was a bit rough, but as I floated to earth, I realized I was smiling. I no longer had any fear of making the jump; I knew I would survive.

One thing I'd never thought about until I started toting my gear around was my physical condition. My rig weighed less than 25 pounds, but no matter whether I was wearing it or carrying it, after a couple of jumps it started getting heavy and breathing became a little more difficult. It wasn't for lack of exercise—I understand sex burns about the same number of calories as a 2-mile hike—it had to be my steady diet of hamburgers, fries, and beer. Whatever the reasons may have been for my poor physical condition, I knew I wasn't capable of running around in the woods with a bag full of money if it came down to evading the Feds on the ground, so I changed my diet and started jogging every morning. Well, I didn't start out jogging—it was more like run a little, walk awhile, then run a little more, but by the end of August I could conformably run 10 miles in an hour and a half, and by the end of September I could run the same 10 miles with a 30-pound backpack in even less time and not even be breathing hard. I wasn't in as good a shape as I was when I worked for Weyerhaeuser and hiked through the woods tending my pot farm, but I figured I could stay ahead of any search team the Feds sent after me, providing they were lucky enough to figure out where I jumped.

I already had over seventy-five jumps under my belt and on Labor Day weekend I logged my first and only nighttime jump prior to the real thing. The night opening was a big deal; in those days not many sport parachutists jumped at night. A safety officer from the United States Parachute Association came out and gave us a lecture on night jumps, warning us about possible vertigo during free fall and how to avoid it by picking out a surface light and keeping an eye on it. I didn't say anything, but I couldn't figure what difference it would make if you had vertigo. Hell, you were going in only one direction after you jumped. But I guess in reality it would be difficult, if not impossible, to differentiate between actually spinning and the sensation of spinning without a reference. When the question came up as to whether or not we could see our canopy or have trouble spotting the landing zone he assured us we would have no problem—we used flashlights to mark our target. The jump went as smooth as silk, no pun intended—prior to nylon, parachutes were made of silk; back then bailing out was referred to as *hitting the silk*.

No questions remained about night openings, I knew I was as ready as I would ever be and it was time to turn my attention to the list of things I considered necessary if I was to be successful in shaking down a yet to be determined airline for two million dollars.

The first thing on my list was the money pouch. When I asked a rigger about making me a canvas pouch with a couple of snap rings sewn onto the zippered side, he asked what I was going to use it for and what size pouch I had in mind. Until he asked the question I hadn't considered how big a stack of hundred-dollar bills it would take to total two million dollars. I told him I was planning to do a little back-country fly-fishing and since I would be spending a couple of weeks hiking and camping in the Cascades I needed something to snap onto the bottom of my pack frame for extra supplies. I told him I would get back to him, but he seemed a bit too curious to suit me so I never contacted him again. Later I found a cobbler who agreed to make the pouch to my specifications without asking too many questions. It took a week to get a couple of snap rings from Parागear, Inc. in Chicago and another week for the cobbler to finish the bag, but in the end it was perfect.

After the rigger brought up the subject of size I went back to Candi's trailer and used one of the many documents she'd collected on the '27 and found that four one-dollar bills would fit perfectly on a piece of regular typing paper with an uncovered strip along the side about 2¼-inches wide. I figured the money would be banded into packets and would not lie as flat as typing paper but surmised the extra 2¼-inch strip would make up the difference. I ran the numbers in my head but assumed I'd made a mistake. By my figures two million dollars in hundred dollar bills would require the space of five thousand sheets of typing paper. I ran the numbers again using a pencil and paper, but still didn't believe the answer. After going over the numbers for a third time I concluded the answer was correct, but I still had a hard time accepting the fact that two million dollars would take up so much space.

To find out just how big a pouch I was going to need I went to Woolworth's and measured the depth of a package of one hundred sheets of typing paper. It was only half an inch high. Not too bad, I thought. Then I realized it would take fifty packages just like the one I'd measured to equal five thousand sheets, which, when stacked one on top of the other, would be over two feet high. This brought to mind the question of weight, and with that, a host of other questions. Would the extra weight and bulk make the jump more difficult? Would it slow me down once I reached the ground?

To answer the weight question I purchased the package of typing paper I'd just measured, walked to a nearby Safeway and dropped the package of typing paper onto the scales in their produce department; it weighed a pound. I could hardly believe it, the money was going to take up 1½ cubic feet and weigh 50 pounds. The reserve parachute that the pouch full of money would replace weighed only 7 or 8 pounds. My entire rig, including the reserve, didn't weigh half that much. I needed to figure a way to make the ransom smaller and easier to conceal. Diamonds could very well be the answer except that I wouldn't know a fake diamond from the real thing if my life depended upon it and besides, it might be impossible to come up with two million dollars in diamonds on short notice. I'd heard about bearer bonds and how they could be cashed at any bank and how they couldn't be traced, but I had a feeling it wasn't that simple. Hell, I didn't even know for sure if there was such a thing as bearer bonds. I figured I'd better stick with hundred-dollar bills and take my chances with the extra weight and bulk. Besides time was ticking away and there were other equally if not more important parts of my plan I hadn't worked out yet. I figured if I could run 20 miles with a 30-pound pack without any problems I would be able to do it with 50 pounds, but just to be safe I added another 10 pounds to my backpack for my run the following morning. As it turned out, due to a change in plans, the money weighed about half my original estimate and required less space.

One very important part was having a device that would convince the captain I was not only serious but also capable of destroying his aircraft and in doing so possibly kill or injure his crew and passengers. Since I was determined not to use a gun, my only logical choice was a bomb or in my case, a fake bomb. Hell, I didn't want the damn thing to go off accidentally and kill me.

I paid six bits for a large attaché case at the Salvation Army thrift store and another two bucks for a piece of electronics equipment with several switches, lots of different-colored wires and weird-looking components. I had no idea what it was used for, neither did the people at the thrift store, but I figured by using some of the switches, wires, and electronic gadgets along with something resembling a few sticks of dynamite or at least something red—in people's minds, all explosive devices are red—I could convince the captain I had a bomb, providing he didn't get too close a look and didn't know anything about explosives.

I worked on the device for the better part of a week and in the end it looked authentic even to me and I knew it was a fake. When I opened the attaché case and showed Candi my handiwork her eyes got real big, she looked a little scared and her voice went up an octave when she asked, almost whispering the question, "Is that a bomb?"

If it was good enough to fool Candi I figured it was good enough to fool the flight crew and went on to other things.

Candi hadn't been coming home nights or weekends for almost a month. I didn't ask her where she was staying or with whom—there was no doubt in my mind the guy knew, after the fact of course, that he'd contributed to the hijacking and probably could have given the authorities enough information to lead them to Candi, but didn't want to admit to how he contributed. We both ignored the obvious. However, I must admit I was a little jealous of the guy; I assumed it was a guy—but hey, who knows? No matter, her sacrifices were paying off. I liked to think of it as a sacrifice, but again, who knows? Every weekday morning she came by the trailer and stayed until midafternoon, during which time we caught up on the things we'd been missing—well, the things I'd been missing anyway. We discussed Operation Quick Rich and talked about all the things we would do with the money.

Candi was a gem, I couldn't have asked for a better partner. She did all the leg work, never complained, and never seemed to tire. I have often wondered what Candi could have achieved and what her life would have been like if, after kicking the habit, she had put as much effort into going back to school and pursuing a legitimate business venture as she put into planning Operation Quick Rich. For that matter, I've wondered a time or two what life would have been like for me had I never left Texas. Candi narrowed her selection of airlines down to two, Pacific Southwest and Northwest Orient. In the end she chose Northwest because of one particular route and the time of day it arrived in Portland.

A few things were still bothering me about the operation. One of my biggest concerns was how to make sure the pilot would follow my instructions and fly no higher than 10,000 feet. I couldn't even be sure he was heading toward Seattle. There was no need to worry, however, as no mountain was too tall for Candi. I discussed the problem with her and the following morning she had the answer:

"Have the pilot fly dirty." She was now spouting aviation terms as though she were a flyer herself.

"What does that mean?"

"It means he'll be flying with the gear and flaps down—he won't be able to fly much faster than 100 knots."

"What about altitude?"

"Have the pilot depressurize, and he'll have to stay below 10,000 feet. It has something to do with the FAA, but to make sure he's following your instructions, you can set your wrist altimeter before takeoff and without cabin pressure you'll get an accurate reading. Once you get the stairs down you can be assured the cabin is no longer pressurized, but be careful, if it is pressurized initially you might get sucked out when you open the door."

Before I had a chance to digest all the information she'd just laid on me she removed a couple of large brown envelopes from her daypack and announced,

"I have some pictures and instructional diagrams on how to open the door and extend the stairs. Also, I have copies of some Jeppesen charts showing the corridors commercial aircraft fly between Portland and Seattle. As long as the pilot remains below 10,000 feet he'll have to stay west of the Cascades, so you'll fly over the area where you're planning to jump without exposing your hand."

We were well into October and time was becoming a factor. Winter wasn't too far away, days were getting shorter, soon the logging industry would start scaling back their operations—after which only a few people would be in the woods. I thought Halloween would be the perfect time, but too many things were still undecided. Candi announced she wouldn't be around for a few days, stating she had made her decision as to the airline, but wanted to ride the route just to make sure.

"What airline did you decide on?"

"I'll tell you when I get back."

Four days later she came home beaming and smiling from ear to ear.

"What?" I asked.

"Northwest Orient!" she explained how she had boarded the flight in Washington, DC and rode it all the way to Seattle.

"Don't worry about a thing, I've got it all figured out." I never did worry about or question any of her decisions during Operation Quick Rich. I knew that in her mind the only way she was ever going to get everything she wanted was for me to be successful in pulling off the hijacking.

With the airline and route decided, I began fine-tuning my plan. Since Halloween had come and gone I decided on Thanksgiving. We checked the almanac and found the sun would set later than I had originally thought, and since my plan was to jump shortly after takeoff I decided to have the money delivered to the Seattle airport, then have the crew fly back to Portland and jump out just before they arrived. I had other reasons for having the money delivered to the Seattle airport rather than Portland. I theorized the time I spent on the ground would work in favor of the Feds, but I would have the advantage while the plane was in the air and figured it would be safer to pass my demands to the crew after they took off from Portland and have the plane remain airborne until the money was ready rather than wait on the ground. I knew that shortly after the captain radioed my demands to the tower, local law enforcement agencies, the FBI, and probably the air force would begin huddling, trying to anticipate my next move and taking steps to head me off at the pass, but surmised they would take a wait-and-see approach. However, I knew they would not hesitate to take quick advantage of any mistakes I made.

By the second week in November we were pretty much set; still, we went over everything almost daily, which led, at Candi's suggestion, to changing destinations for the pilot and crew after I had the money.

"If you have them fly back to Portland and you're not on board when they land they'll know you're still in Washington State and somewhere along their flight path, which would make things a lot easier for a search team. Why not have them think you want to get out of the country and tell them to fly to Mexico City?"

"That's good, I like it."

Keeping warm was a problem I hadn't solved and it was beginning to weigh heavily on my mind. By the end of November temperatures could be down near freezing in Washington and Oregon, in which case I suspected it would be below zero at 10,000 feet. Also, chances were it would be raining, which meant snow, sleet, or even hail at any altitude above 1000 feet. I figured I could survive the cold and even rain, sleet, or snow during my descent; I wouldn't be in the air much longer than two and a half to three minutes, four minutes at the outside. I planned to free-fall the first 7,000 feet, which would take less than forty seconds. The remaining 3,000 feet would take somewhere between two to three minutes. (An open canopy drops at around 1000 feet per minute) The problem would be after I reached the ground; if I got wet and cold while in the air and was unable to change into warm, dry clothes, or find a way to warm up and dry out I stood a good chance of dying of hypothermia. I thought about using a neoprene dry suit, but figured it would be too bulky to wear underneath a suit and might attract unwanted attention before I boarded the airplane. I knew wool would keep me warm even when wet; I also knew layering was better than one bulky garment, so when I heard about "Broadway Joe" (Namath) wearing pantyhose under his uniform during games I figured I'd use pantyhose and wool long johns. When I asked Candi to pick me up a couple of pair of pantyhose she gave me a weird look. When I explained to her what I had in mind she said, "Tights and a leotard will serve you better than pantyhose."

"Tights and a what?"

"A leotard. I wore them to ballet when I was a little girl. I'll pick up a couple of sets for you." She giggled. "What color do you want?"

I kept an eye on suits at the thrift store until a fairly nice one, a size larger than I would have normally worn, showed up on the rack. It was a bit dated, but otherwise a good-looking suit. Candi picked up two sets of long wool underwear to go with the tights and leotards. I had already purchased a hat, a raincoat, a pair of loafers, a dress shirt and tie; now with the suit my wardrobe was complete. I figured it would be pretty easy to pass myself off as a businessman going home for the weekend and no one would give me a second look until I made my demands known. Then they would take notice but it would be too late—I would already be on board with a bomb and a plane full of hostages. I found myself smiling as I visualized the expressions on various faces when told of my demands and the questions they would ask.

"He has what? He wants what?"

Almost daily I went over the list of equipment I thought would be either useful or necessary. I kept changing my mind, adding things on occasion while scratching others and sometimes adding items I'd eliminated previously, but when it came down to the final list I'd eliminated everything but a pair of lightweight field boots made from green kangaroo leather by Browning—I would have preferred a pair of heavy-duty jump boots, but I needed to conserve on weight—ski goggles, a wristwatch, a wool pullover ski mask, and for emergency use on the ground a magnesium fire starter kit, and a Swiss Army knife. For a compass I chose the SILVA Ranger. Hopefully, I would need none of the last three items. The last two items to be eliminated were an Altimaster II and a Mallory pen light with side-by-side batteries. Originally, I had intended to tape the pen light to my arm so I could see my altimeter, but since I wouldn't be able to tell if I was over a hill or a valley when I jumped I figured it would be safer to wait until I spotted some lights before jumping, then use the lights as a ground reference. I would count the seconds of free fall as a backup measure—I practiced every day until I could count off a minute with no more than a one-second error ten times in a row. I was ready, we were both ready, we had spent a lot of time and energy preparing, we had planned down to the very last detail; it was time to get it on, but there were still a few loose ends to tie up.

A week before Thanksgiving we drove down to Portland and rented a room in a fleabag hotel, as husband and wife, for two weeks and paid in advance. Next we drove to the airport and bought two round-trip tickets to Hawaii, again masquerading as husband and wife. From there we drove back to Tacoma and transferred everything we owned, except the two bags we'd left in our hotel room in Portland, from the trailer to the camper. We had already given notice we'd be moving out of the trailer so there were no problems when we turned in the keys and left early Saturday morning.

At the local flea market we sold everything at giveaway prices. Again, except for two bags, whatever they offered was good enough. The few things no one wanted we dumped into a trash barrel. From the flea market I drove to a car lot sporting a big sign stating, "We buy used cars and trucks at fair prices."

The guy was a shyster, but I didn't care. I just wanted to make sure we didn't leave anything around to give someone a reason to start looking for us and perhaps connect me with the hijacking, such as an abandoned vehicle or personal property in a trailer with rent overdue. I agreed to the shyster's price with the stipulation he pay me in cash and take us to the airport. At the price he was paying I knew he would agree. I also knew he would lie about the price he paid when it came down to paying his taxes. He would add at least a thousand dollars to the price he actually paid in order to show less profit on his tax return. Again, I didn't care, I was just tying up loose ends.

I had the guy drop us at a hotel near SeaTac, where we reserved a room for two nights. We left our bags in the room and then walked to the airport. Candi bought a round-trip ticket to Missoula on Northwest Orient, and half an hour later I bought a round-trip ticket to Portland, I was scheduled to return a month later. I had no intention of using the return portion of the ticket; it was just another ruse to throw any would-be investigator off our scent. We walked back to our hotel and, except for meals, we didn't venture outside our room until Monday morning. We boarded the plane separately and sat in different rows, Candi checked one of the bags we'd kept and hand-carried the other. I had nothing to check or carry. I wouldn't see Candi again until

Wednesday evening and even then we wouldn't speak or indicate we knew each other in any way whatsoever.

It was early Wednesday afternoon when Candi boarded Northwest Orient flight 305, found an aisle seat in row 15, and stowed her bag under the seat. To say Candi was apprehensive would be an understatement—she was sitting on pins and needles, well aware that everything depended on her. She almost wet her panties when a passing stewardess hesitated and cast a cursory eye in the direction of her carry-on bag. However, her emotions were not outwardly visible, and no one observing her actions or reactions would have guessed or even suspected she was the key to tomorrow's headlines.

Candi took a deep breath and sank back into her seat as the pilot rotated the 727 and pointed its nose skyward. It was the first time in six months she'd had a chance to relax—her part in a plan she'd first thought would never work was almost finished. The rest would be up to DB. She had first thought DB was just trying to impress her with a lot of talk when he explained his plan to her—men trying to impress her for personal gain was nothing new to Candi. But DB was different. Oh, he talked the talk right enough, but he was also the kind of guy who walked the walk; she had made a good choice when she picked DB out of a crowd of potential losers to be her personal savior. She regretted some of the things she'd done in exchange for information on the '27. It wasn't that she hadn't done them all before in times past, but now she felt she owed DB. It wasn't that she loved him, but she did feel she owed him her respect, and with that came a vague sense of loyalty and remorse. She closed her eyes and drifted off to sleep dreaming of how she would live the rest of her life. She flashed back to her childhood—she did that often. She'd been happy growing up in La Jolla until that fatal summer when she was lured away from it all by the rhetoric and pipe dreams of the new socialists, but now she was about to get it all back with interest. Candi believed money could buy her all the things she had missed since running away from home, and to her way of thinking, two million dollars would buy a lot of happiness. She didn't realize, and it may have been insignificant, that DB was not center stage in her dreams as one might have expected. He wasn't even in the wings.

Walking the Walk

It was the first time I'd had a chance to sleep late in several weeks. It was almost noon by the time I shaved, showered, and finished dressing. I didn't know when I would have another chance to eat, so I walked a few blocks to the greasy spoon where I'd eaten two hamburgers, a double order of fries, and a bowl of chili the night before and ate two more burgers with double fries.

It was after one o'clock when I got back to the hotel and began laying out my gear. I double-checked everything against the list I was carrying in my wallet. The only thing remaining to be done was to write the note I intended to give to the captain. I would do that at the airport. I hadn't prepared the note earlier in case of an accident, a search by the police, or any other possible reason someone might get a look at it and either ask questions, call the authorities or remember seeing if after the fact. I dressed slowly—next to my skin were the tights and leotard, next came a set of long wool underwear, then a second pair of tights and another leotard followed by more long underwear. I slipped on knee-high silk stockings followed by a pair of heavy wool socks, pulled on my trousers, tucked in my shirt, clipped on and adjusted my tie, donned my jacket, and stepped into my loafers. Then I dropped my wallet, containing only a couple of hundred dollars—all other money and ID I'd left with Candi—along with an envelope and a pair of sunglasses into my pocket, slipped on a raincoat, set a hat on my head and pulled it down tight. I took a quick look in the mirror and smiled my approval—I was ready. I picked up my attaché case, walked out into the passageway and closed the door, checking to make sure it locked.

Several blocks away, at another hotel, I walked into the lobby, told the desk clerk I needed to get to the airport, and asked if he would mind calling me a cab.

I arrived at the airport earlier than I had originally planned, but I was getting antsy and figured it was better to arrive too early than too late. I paid the driver and added what I guessed was the average tip—I didn't want to give him a reason to remember me by tipping too much or too little. A composite sketch would no doubt appear in the morning papers and would probably make the late night news. I was counting on the hat, raincoat, and lack of glasses to keep the cabby from connecting me to the fare he picked up at the hotel. Hopefully, the hotel clerk would not make the connection either. Even if they did recognize me, it is unlikely the Feds would connect a clean-shaven guy in a business suit with a pot-growing deserter passing himself off as a hippie living with a hanger-on flower child.

Although relatively calm, I was a bit nervous and ill at ease. I hoped it wasn't too obvious to the casual observer. I may not have been as cool as Hardin had been during his attempt to commandeer a military aircraft, but my problem was heat, not a loss of nerve. It wasn't a hot day by any means—the temperature was around fifty—but I was sweating to the point where I was dripping wet underneath my clothes. All the layering was working too well. I took off the raincoat and draped it over my arm; it didn't give me much relief from the heat and probably contributed to a huge error on my part when purchasing my ticket to Seattle. Being uncomfortably warm was only part of the problem I was dealing with—my thoughts were consumed with Candi and what might happen after we had the money.

I had no doubt Candi still believed, just as she had stated early on, I was her last chance and she would do whatever was necessary to make sure I was always there for her. That is not to say her feelings for me were not real and the favors she bestowed upon me so passionately were not heartfelt, but I also knew the love in our relationship was a one-way street. There would never be any legal documents binding us together, but there was something about Candi that made me want to take care of her and I knew I was tied to her, for better or worse, until destiny took its course. I had always doubted Candi was capable of true love or even understood the concept, and suspected whatever loyalty she had for me was tied to her own survival. I knew the bottom line. I could be replaced. In my heart I didn't want to believe it but my gut told me I should always keep the bottom line in mind, if for no other reason than that I knew her many moods. Candi could be as cold and ruthless as the most hardened criminal I'd ever known and I feared there might come a time when she would leave me lying on the sidewalk bleeding to death just as she'd left her husband back in Denver. She would do it without emotion.

The mistake I'd made wasn't anything that would jeopardize me during the execution of my plan, but it might send the authorities off in the right direction to look for the perpetrator. Not only was I burning up from all the layers of clothing and sweating profusely as I approached the ticket agent, I was agonizing over the decision I had to make in regards to Candi and the money. I just wanted to get my ticket and get outside where I could cool off a little and think, so when the counter attendant asked, "What's your name?" My military service kicked in and I automatically answered,

"Cooper?"

In the military everyone is required to fill out forms for just about everything, almost daily, and all forms begin with a block for your name and ask for your last name, first name, and middle initial.

Realizing my mistake, I recovered quickly and gave him a first name I had used many times before and said. "Dan" I repeated the name for the attendant's benefit, "Dan Cooper."

Outside I thought about it for a minute or two and decided it wasn't likely to be a problem since I would never use the name D. B. Cooper again; our hotel room and tickets to Hawaii were in the name of my dead navy shipmate from Wyoming. The driver's license, social security card, and birth certificate I carried were also in the name of my old biking buddy; Candi and I even had a fake marriage license with his name on it. The one thing driving me crazy for the last couple of weeks, which now tended to dominate my thinking, was the thought of losing Candi. I figured with two million dollars in her hot little hands she would be long gone in a matter of weeks or even days. Lately, anytime we weren't discussing or planning Operation Quick Rich she'd talked about the things *she* would do after she had *her* money. Never once did I hear the word *we* in her plans. Perhaps it was selfishness on my part, but I figured if we had enough money to live comfortably for a while, although nothing approaching two million dollars, she wouldn't take a chance on abandoning me and going off on her own. When the money got low again, I'd come up with another get-rich scheme. Okay, so I was selfish in wanting to keep her around, but I knew that no amount of money was going to buy back the life she had thrown away. But, without having, if only for a while, some semblance of what she perceived her life would have been had she stayed in La Jolla, she would never be happy. It may have been a misconception on my part, but if her stories were true then she was happier with me than she'd been with anyone in a very long time.

Sitting on the toilet I rested the attaché on my knees, removed the pen and paper from the envelope I'd been carrying in my pocket and began printing the note I would give a crew member to pass on to the captain. I told myself I was doing Candi a favor by asking for two hundred thousand in twenty-dollar bills rather than the two million we had agreed upon. Oh, Candi was part of the reason all right, but I wasn't all that sure the airline would give me two million dollars or how much time it would take to round up that much money even if the local CEOs had the go-ahead from the president of Northwest Orient. To me it seemed the safest deal all the way around. Two hundred thousand was nothing to Northwest Orient. They wouldn't take a chance on getting someone hurt or killed for such a trivial amount. Also, it was just about impossible to spend a hundred-dollar bill without someone carefully scrutinizing it to make sure it wasn't counterfeit. Oftentimes they recorded the serial number and occasionally asked for identification; there was no doubt in my mind someone would record the serial numbers on at least some of the bills. Each time we spent one of the bills whose number had been recorded we'd drop a bread crumb, and like the birds in Hansel and Gretel the Feds would follow the trail of bread crumbs no matter where it led them. Unless we were very careful, and had luck on our side the trail of crumbs would eventually lead them to us. On the other hand, nobody would give a second glance at a twenty-dollar bill, much less record the serial number or ask for identification.

Candi would have a hissy when I showed up with only two hundred thousand, but she'd get over it. I figured I'd lie and tell her I accidentally left off a zero when I wrote the note. I knew she wouldn't believe me, but I knew Candi, and two hundred thousand dollars would go a long way in smoothing her ruffled feathers. After she counted the two hundred grand a couple of times she'd forget all about wanting two million.

Waiting to board the airplane was the worst part. Minutes seemed like hours. I tried to act nonchalant and kept to myself as much as possible, but the longer I waited the worse it got. I wondered if Hardin had had preboarding jitters. Not likely. He just walked onto the aircraft with an M-16 and demanded the crew take him to Da Nang. For me it wasn't that simple.

The plane finally arrived and passengers terminating in Portland were disembarking while those bound for Seattle remained on board and although they didn't know it, they were about to become witnesses to a historical event. Actually, the flight was pretty much on time, but if anyone had asked me I would've told them it was way overdue. I watched Candi enter the lounge. She looked at me just once, very briefly, to make sure I was there and that I saw her. She sat down for no more than ten seconds while she laced and retied her shoes. When she left I walked over, sat down in the same chair, and peeled the piece of masking tape from underneath the arm of the chair. I turned it over and smiled. Written on the tape was the numeral fifteen. I rolled the masking tape into a little ball and dropped it into my pocket.

When the call came for passengers to board and I walked toward the ramp I realized I was no longer anxious or uneasy; all my emotions were under control. I spotted the bag underneath the isle seat in row fifteen and sat down momentarily before moving the bag to my assigned row. I made a cursory check of the contents to make sure everything was still there. Just knowing all the hard work and planning was about to pay off served to bolster my confidence. The only hurdle left was takeoff and from then on it would be all downhill.

About fifteen minutes after we were airborne I attempted to pass my note to the crew. But when I handed the note to a stewardess, rather than read it, the dumb bitch put it in her pocket. It took a lot of hand signals before I got her attention and succeeded in getting her to look at the note. After reading it she huddled with another stewardess for a few seconds before getting on the phone and following a brief discussion with whoever was at the other end made a beeline for the cockpit.

I smiled knowing I had anticipated their every move; it wouldn't be long before the captain would show up. I moved to a window seat so as to make a seat available to the captain. I knew he would want to get a look at me, take a look at the bomb and generally feel me out to see if I was a rational person, serious about blowing up his airplane if my demands weren't met, or if I was just hopped up, out of control, and bluffing. Either way, he had no choice; he had to talk with me firsthand to find out what kind of a person he was dealing with.

A few minutes passed before the stewardess came back and asked to look at the bomb. I opened the attaché case just long enough to give her a glimpse inside. She hurried back to the phone and reported what she'd seen.

A little more time passed before the captain came back, sat down beside me, looked me over, and asked about the bomb. I opened the attaché case long enough for him to see it, but not long enough for him to try and identify any parts. I told him I was serious and that I didn't want him to land until they had the money and the parachutes ready for us on the ground. I demanded two rigs (four parachutes); however, the parachutes were meant to deceive whomever was in charge and lure them into a false sense of security. I had no intention of using either of the rigs. There was a possibility the parachutes would be packed in a way to cause them to malfunction, have beacons attached, or both, but I suspected the parachutes would be packed properly since there was a chance that deliberately rigging the canopy to malfunction would be considered premeditated murder. But I had no doubt they'd be set up with beacons and if I was dumb enough to use one, helicopters with searchlights would show up a few minutes after I pulled the ripcord.

The captain asked if I wanted him to circle, I told him I wanted him to circle until the money and parachutes were ready. The interview—I guess that's what you would call it—was brief and the captain returned to the cockpit. That was the last contact I had with him except via the intercom. From then on our conversations were shuttled back and forth by a stewardess.

It was well over two hours before the stewardess informed me the money and parachutes were ready and said the captain wanted to know if they could land. I told her he could land, but to make sure he parked in an isolated but well-lighted area. Next, she said the captain wanted to know if the passengers could get off. I told her they could go. Then she asked if the crew could go, I told her they were to stay on board, that we still had some flying to do. She asked if all the crew had to stay. I figured the fewer people on board the fewer I had to keep an eye on, so I told her everyone could go except the cockpit crew and one stewardess, I pointed a finger at her. "You."

"Me?" She didn't appear overly concerned, but she had a why-me look about her. I repeated the word so there would be no misunderstanding,

"You." She looked at me for several seconds as though waiting for me to change my mind, then resigned herself to the task and went to inform the captain.

Sometime later she returned to tell me the parachutes had arrived and wanted to know how close the delivery vehicle could come. I looked out the window and indicated a lighted area near the wingtip where they could park. I told her only one guy could approach the airplane, he was not to come on board but could deliver them to her on the back stairs.

I don't know if the stewardess was just uneasy or she was getting a little turned on by the excitement, but she asked if I was going to make someone jump with me. It had never crossed my mind and it seemed strange to me that anybody would even consider that I would take a hostage. The last thing I wanted was to have someone with me on the ground. However, I couldn't see anything wrong with letting them think taking a hostage was a possibility, since it would give them something to think about. So rather than giving her a definite yes or no, I told her maybe, and left it at that. She didn't inquire any further; she probably assumed or was perhaps hoping it would be her—I think she had taken a liking to me.

A short time later the same vehicle showed up with the money and delivered it the same way they delivered the parachutes. I looked inside the bag and checked a few bundles, I didn't think whoever was running the show for Northwest Orient would try and stiff me at this stage in the game, but I checked anyway. I had grown tired of a-go-between so when the stewardess asked where I wanted to go, I took the phone from her and told the guy on the other end I wanted to go to Mexico City. I don't know if that took them by surprise or not—they discussed it for a few seconds and said it was okay with them, but we would have to refuel somewhere along the way. After some discussion, I agreed to refuel in Reno, and then I was told in order to reach Reno we would have to refuel before taking off. I didn't care where they refueled—thirty minutes after the pilot rotated I would no longer be on board, but I didn't want them to suspect that I intended to bail out shortly after takeoff so I agreed to let them refuel, providing one man could do it by himself. I suspect, however, they had a pretty good idea the destination was not Mexico City or even Reno, since my demands were to maintain an altitude below 10,000 feet, to fly with the wheels and flaps down, and to not pressurize the cabin. Flying dirty would not let the captain cross over the Cascades and force him to fly, according to the Jeppesen Charts, one of two corridors. His choices would be to fly either over Portland or a few miles east of Portland, either way they would pass over the area where I intended to jump.

Little delays were beginning to add up and I had the feeling I was getting jerked around. My plan was to be out of the plane and on the ground no later than three hours after I made my demands known to the captain, so I got on the horn and told the captain not to try and stall me and he shouldn't push me too far. The captain did his best to convince me he wasn't stalling or trying to push me, but I knew they were lying when they asked if somebody from FAA could come on board. I suspected the guy wasn't from the Federal Aviation Association, but some FBI hitter with a big gun in his pocket and several tricks up his sleeve. I told them in no uncertain terms the guy could not come on board and that I'd had enough waltzing around, there were to be no more delays and they'd better get the show on the road.

I instructed the stewardess to go into the cockpit and lock the door, and then pulled the carry-on bag Candi had left underneath the seat and took out my LOPO rig, money pouch, green kangaroo boots, ski goggles, wool pullover ski mask, magnesium fire starter kit, Swiss Army knife, and compass. I put my boots on first and then transferred the money to the pouch, stuck the knife, fire starter kit, and compass into a small zippered pocket at one end of the money pouch, then using the snap rings I fastened the pouch onto my rig where normally the reserve parachute would have attached. I pulled on the wool ski mask and set the goggles on my head just above my eyes.

I had gone over the instructions on how to open the door and extend the stairs with the stewardess earlier to make sure nothing had changed since Candi obtained operational diagrams and step-by-step instructions on how to operate the door and stairs. I had memorized the procedure to the point I could do it in my sleep, but I figured it wouldn't hurt to double-check. The stewardess had told me she didn't think it would open in the air, I don't know if she seriously suspected it wouldn't open or was just giving me something to think about. I told her it would open.

Remembering Candi's warning about getting sucked out if the airplane was pressurized I cut some shroud line from one of the parachutes the airline had delivered and tethered myself to the last row of seats. The stairs opened as advertised, but would not stay down due to pressure created by air passing underneath the fuselage at a 100 knots or better, so I took the other, still intact, parachute rig and walked down the stairs until they came down a bit and jammed the rig in between the stairs and the airplane just below where it hinged. This did not keep the stairs down very far, but it was enough to allow me to see through the opening.

I was surprised when the captain's voice came over the loudspeaker and asked if there was anything they could do for me. I guess he was hoping something had caused me to change my mind. I considered ignoring him, but figured someone might come out to see what was going on if I didn't respond, I didn't want them to realize I wasn't using one of the parachutes provided by the airline, so I answered, "No."

I didn't want to aid the investigators by leaving something on board that might help them figure out who made off with Northwest Orient's money, so I started throwing stuff overboard. I had managed to get the note back; I tore it into little pieces, stuck it down into the toe of one of my loafers and threw the loafers down the stairs—I knew the scraps of paper would be sucked out of the shoe by the airplane's turbulence and scattered in all directions. Next I stuffed the raincoat, hat, and sunglasses into the bag Candi had used to bring my gear on board and threw it down the stairs. The last things to go were the fake bomb and the parachute cord I'd used for a tether. And then I removed my tie, turned up the collar on my jacket, strapped on my LOPO, adjusted the ski goggles over my eyes, and duckwalked toward the stairs.

Murphy's Law Rules

Someone once said, be careful what you ask for, you may get it. I had wanted a dark night to make it difficult for anyone in a chase plane to spot me when I jumped; however, I'd gotten a lot more than I'd asked for. There was a new moon, which would have been nothing more than a sliver of light in the western sky had it been visible. A new moon with starlight would have been perfect—even though it would have enabled me to see and check my canopy for problems, given me a good view of the landscape, and allowed me to identify landmarks below, it would have been very difficult for anyone to spot me. With only a new moon and starlight it would have been next to impossible to spot me during free fall, and their chances of spotting me after my parachute opened wouldn't have been much better. Searching for me once I reached the ground would have been an exercise in futility.

The clouds appearing as dense fog while the rain flowed in little rippling sheets across the cabin windows made it impossible for me to spot anything on the ground; at times I could barely see the marker lights on the wings. The view from the top of the stairs wasn't any better, so I eased down the first couple of steps and hunkered down, but was still unable to spot anything on the ground. The fact that my night vision was shot because of lights inside the airplane didn't help. I should have worn red-tinted glasses instead of the dark ones—red glasses filtered out the white light that temporarily destroyed night vision.

I checked my wristwatch. I was thankful I still had my old Timex with its uranium painted hands and numerals. I had hoped to be on the ground within three hours after announcing my intentions to the crew, but figured anything under four hours would be okay. The time frame was good; just a little over three hours had passed since I passed the note to the stewardess. A little unsettling though, was the fact that I didn't know how far we'd come since takeoff. I had a general idea but didn't know exactly, since I had no way of knowing our ground speed. Candi had insisted by forcing the pilot to fly dirty his airspeed wouldn't be much in excess of 100 knots, if that fast. Airspeed and ground speed, however, were not one and the same. Almost thirty minutes had passed since take-off, but if I figured our airspeed at 100 knots the average speed would be less since I would need to compensate for the time it had taken the pilot to acquire speed and altitude after takeoff. Also, without knowing wind velocity and direction it would be impossible to figure ground speed. I was getting concerned—no, I was a bit beyond concerned, although nowhere near panic. I knew I should have been out of the airplane and on the ground already, but I had no way of knowing the lay of the land underneath me or how far above the terrain we were flying, and I didn't want to jump without something for a reference.

I found myself wishing I hadn't eliminated the Altimaster II and Mallory pen light. I quickly put the thought out of my mind. I wasn't going to be distracted by doubt or start second-guessing myself this late in the game. Besides, my wrist altimeter would be of little value since it was barometric and could not have been referenced to the ground below me. To get the exact distance would require a radar altimeter like the one in the cockpit; otherwise I wouldn't know whether I was flying over a mountain or a valley. Normally, before taking off, a pilot called the tower for the present barometric pressure and set the reading into the altimeter, in which case his reference to zero would be sea level. In sport parachuting you ignored the barometric pressure and reference your altimeter to zero at the drop zone. This gave you an accurate reading when you jumped. If I had referenced my altimeter to zero before takeoff it would be of little value to me since I would have no way of knowing the difference between the elevation of the ground underneath me and the airport. I considered calling the captain and asking for a reading on his radar altimeter, but just then I spotted several bright lights through a hole in the clouds. Relieved at having spotted a reference point I moved down the stairs for a better look.

It has been my experience as long as I can remember, no matter how well or how long I planned for an event or happening, something seemed to go wrong every time and it always happened when I least expected it. Nothing had changed; Murphy's Law still ruled my life. I walked down the stairs, preparing to jump, my mind totally focused on the task at hand. First and of utmost importance, was surviving the jump and reaching the ground uninjured; second, to spend as little time in the air as possible. I figured my safest bet was to cannonball upon exiting and remain in that position until I slowed down, shift to a modified cannonball until I stabilized, then go into a head-down dive toward the lights counting off the seconds until it was time to open my canopy. Although I would be using the lights as a reference to determine when to pull the rip cord it was necessary to count off the seconds so as to not become hypnotized by the lights and open too late or not at all. As I eased my way down the stairs, my weight overcame the air pressure and the bottom end of the stairs began to fall away from the airplane, becoming lower with each step I took. Near the bottom of the stairs the wind made it difficult to hold on and the noise was so deafening it was difficult to concentrate. I had just reached the bottom step and was about to make my exit when the parachute I'd used to prevent the air pressure from keeping the stairs closed fell free, was picked up by the wind and hurled aft. It slammed into my right shoulder with the force of a Brahma bull crashing into a loading chute, knocking me off the stairs into a cold, wet, pitch-black sky.

In the dark, I couldn't be sure, but I think there was a mixture of rain, sleet, and snow. Whatever it was pelted me like sand in a west Texas dust storm, causing intense pain. I couldn't begin to guess the temperature, but freezing cold immediately penetrated all the way to the bone, turning the perspiration in my clothing into what felt like ice against my skin. I put the weather conditions and my discomfort out of mind and concentrated on stabilizing. I was tumbling and spinning out of control, but managed to tuck into a cannonball and began to slow down, although I was still tumbling and spinning out of control. I couldn't tell how much I'd slowed, but I knew I had to stabilize and went into the modified cannonball with my head up, elbows out with a slightly looser tuck. As I began to stabilize, I eased my arms out and my legs back. Within a few seconds I was in complete control and went into a headlong dive. All the time and money I'd spent on training had paid off; I had been correct in my thinking when I determined it would be suicide to try this jump without being properly prepared. Even today, there is no doubt in my mind, had I been unfamiliar with parachutes and sport parachuting, I would have died that night. In all likelihood I would have impacted the ground without opening my canopy.

I had lost my concentration when the parachute knocked me off the stairs and it was several seconds before I collected my wits and focused on my first objective, surviving. Even without the extra problem of exiting unexpectedly and without having my intended course of action set clearly in my mind, the jump was a lot more hazardous than I'd anticipated. Unlike the light Cessna we'd used at Pacific Parachute Center in Aurora, the 727's slipstream, not to mention the jet's exhaust, was something to be reckoned with beyond anything I had previously experienced. Even if the exit had gone perfectly, it is unlikely that I would have been able to maintain complete control in the very beginning, although I have no doubt I would have recovered more quickly and wouldn't have neglected to begin counting off seconds the moment I exited. Surviving was still my primary objective and at the moment it took on a new meaning; not being spotted seemed a moot point. The clouds had closed in again and the hole through which I'd spotted the lights no longer existed. It was hard to ignore the freezing cold and the pain from being pelted with rain, sleet, or whatever, but my biggest problem was not knowing how long I'd been in the air. I figured somewhere between fifteen and twenty seconds had passed since I'd been knocked off the stairs, which meant in another twenty to twenty-five seconds I would become a permanent part of the landscape. I started counting off seconds. It was then that a heart-stopping thought popped into my mind. What if the pilot was flying well below 10,000 feet? And what if I'd underestimated the time between being knocked off the stairs and the time I started counting seconds of free fall? What if both scenarios were in play? Without considering the circumstances any further I flared to slow my descent and then brought both hands in, grabbed the handle with my right hand and yanked—a movement with your free hand equal to the one pulling the rip cord is necessary in order to maintain stability until your canopy opens. My fingers were so cold I could barely grip the handle.

Again, my training proved well worth the time and effort. During the couple of heartbeats between the time I pulled my ripcord and my canopy opened I popped through the clouds less than 300 feet above the ground. Had I hesitated, even for another second, it is unlikely my canopy would have opened in time. The first 1000 feet of free fall takes about ten seconds, thereafter you free-fall at about 1000 feet every five seconds. I was still freezing, but the sleet and snow that pelted me on exiting the airplane had become just a light rain near the ground. Hundreds, maybe thousands of lights glowed through the mist, they were everywhere I looked. I was so puzzled by all the lights it was several seconds before I realized I was looking at Portland and Vancouver. I knew I had jumped later than I should have, but I couldn't believe I was so far off target. When I had seen the lights through the hole in the clouds I assumed them to be the lights around Ariel Dam, which meant I was right where I wanted to be, the Lewis River, an area I knew like the back of my hand due to my pot farming and employment with Weyerhaeuser. With my thinking totally consumed by the odd turn of events, I forgot I was drifting earthward at about 16 feet per second—an open 26-foot canopy falls at about 1000 feet per minute. By the time I regained my senses and began checking the area for a safe place to land I realized I was only a 100 feet above the Columbia River. It was too late to consider options— no amount of pulling on risers would affect the glide path of my canopy enough to clear the river.

My mind raced over the procedures for a water entry: release leg straps, release chest strap, and fold arms so as not to fall out of your harness, then as you feel your feet enter the water, put your arms straight up over your head and slip out of your harness—this will most likely keep you from getting tangled in your parachute, which might make the difference between drowning or getting out of the water alive. My hands were so cold there was no feeling in my fingers and I had trouble squeezing the snap rings to release my leg straps, but finally succeeded and had just sat back in my harness—a parachute harness is designed so you actually sit, rather than dangle underneath your canopy—and was preparing to release the chest strap when the water closed over my head. Luckily, the current carried the parachute downstream faster than it carried me, so when I surfaced I was clear of the canopy and shroud lines. Upon entering the water the parachute quickly became heavy with silt and began to sink, I managed to release my chest strap and free myself from the harness and had just started to swim away when I remembered the money. I turned around, but I was too late—the parachute had either sunk or floated away. I swam in the direction of the current, hoping to spot the canopy, but again the dark night I had wished for had worked against me. Nothing was visible and I couldn't feel the canopy or any shroud lines underneath the surface. To say I regretted not having Capewells was an understatement. Capewells would have enabled me to disconnect from the canopy upon entering the water, in which case I would still be wearing the harness with the money pouch attached. I uttered a string of curses, damning the river, the night, the weather, everything and everyone I could think of, pounded my fists into the water several times, then gave up and headed for shore.

Bad News

I've always found it strange the way the mind works, especially in times of crisis when an unrelated thought dominates your thinking. I risked my life hijacking a commercial airliner, survived a parachute jump never tried before and under the worst possible conditions, was freezing to death in the middle of the Columbia River, or at best about to drown because I was barely able to move my arms and legs enough to keep afloat—and the only thing I could think about was how I was going to tell Candi I didn't have the money.

We had planned everything so well and put so much time and effort into our Operation Quick Rich scheme it should have worked. Hell, it did work—it worked perfectly and just as planned. I got the money, jumped out of an airplane at 10,000 feet, and survived. Nevertheless, I was in the middle of the Columbia River without the money and about to drown. If I had exited the airplane one second later I could have walked back to the hotel; it just didn't seem fair. I let go another string of curses and made a feeble attempt to pound my fist against the river's surface again. And still, even faced with the possibility of dying, the only thing on my mind was how to explain my failure to Candi. I knew I couldn't continue to focus on this particular question, at least for the moment, or I would die.

Although the water seemed relatively warm compared to the freezing weather at 10,000 feet, I knew it was sucking heat out of my body at a much faster rate than the mixture of rain, sleet, and snow I had encountered upon exiting the airplane. If I didn't make it to shore pretty soon and figure out some way to get warm and dry I would die of hypothermia and my problem of explaining things to Candi would be moot. Not only was it difficult to move my arms and legs, but silt was collecting in my clothes, which made it even more difficult to stay afloat. I removed my jacket and shirt without too much trouble, but in order to get my trousers off I had to first remove my boots, which wasn't so easy. The advantage of navy bellbottoms, designed to be easily pulled off without your having to remove your shoes in case you fell overboard, flashed through my mind. I had double-tied my laces and it took considerable effort and concentration to get the knots loose. Even though I was in pretty good shape—I was thankful for having the foresight to get myself in good physical condition by starting a running program—by the time I managed to remove my trousers I was just about out of energy and was beginning to consider the possibility that I might not get out of the river alive. For the first time in my life I knew the meaning of fear. I was on the verge of panic when something profound happened—a memory from the past saved my life.

One of my theories, that everything you have learned since birth is stored in your brain, was reinforced with another flashback to my navy days. Although it is difficult and sometimes impossible to recall a particular name or event on demand—we've all used that "It's right on the tip of my tongue" phrase—solutions to problems are often recalled automatically in times of desperation. One of the things we had to do, in boot camp, was to jump from a 30-foot diving platform into a swimming pool and convert our clothes into flotation devices. I thought I had long forgotten the words of the instructor, a chief petty officer who, as a seaman during World War II, had survived six days in the water after being blown overboard when a direct hit by a Japanese dive bomber resulted in the explosion of his ship's magazine. Some trip mechanism in my brain took me back to boot camp. The chief seemed to be looking directly at me and his words were ringing in my ears.

"Never give up and you can survive—give up and you die." At that moment the chief's words were even more inspiring than they were the day I heard them. They provided me with newfound energy and a desire to live beyond anything I had ever known before. Give up—hell no, I wasn't about to give up, I had everything to gain by living and everything to lose by dying. I knew surviving would be a one-step-at-a-time procedure and I concentrated solely on tying knots in the bottoms of my trouser legs. With the knots pulled as tight as my strength and numb fingers would allow, I closed the zipper and managed to slip the button through the proper hole in the waistband. Next, with both hands on the waistband and while kicking hard to stay afloat, I held the trousers above and behind my head before bringing them forward and down against the water with all the strength my weakened condition could provide. With this action I managed to trap a considerable amount of air inside the trousers. I continued to add to my makeshift life preserver by filling my lungs, and then ducking underneath the surface and expelling air inside the trousers. As the legs filled with air the trousers began to take on the look of what I imagined water wings to be, and by gathering the waistband and holding it closed with one hand I was able to ease onto the trousers. The inflated legs, although mostly submerged, stuck out in front of my shoulders about a foot, requiring only a light slow kick to stay afloat. I suddenly realized I was relaxed and smiling. I didn't know why, but I found myself smiling at the weirdest times. I'd heard about laughing in the face of danger—my subconscious smiles seemed to come after I'd managed to avoid disaster. I wasn't out of the woods yet, or in this case the river, but I had no doubt I would make it. I wanted to shout my gratitude to my old boot camp instructor, but knowing no one would hear me and not wanting to waste the energy, I merely whispered, "Thanks, Chief, I owe you one."

With my confidence restored, I gathered my wits about me and made a quick survey of my situation. The current was faster than I had first realized, which was working in my favor since it was taking me toward the Washington side of the river. I held the waistband of my trousers closed with one hand so as not to let the air escape, and began dog-paddling toward the riverbank with the other hand while kicking as hard as I could.

Mother Nature had declared war on me or so it seemed. She gathered her forces and launched her attack against me the moment I exited the aircraft and by all indications had no intention of letting up. I was still several yards from shore when my knee collided with a sharp rock that laid the flesh open to the bone; then when I finally managed to climb onto the bank I found myself in the middle of a briar patch. I had one of two choices—I could go back into the river and float past the briar patch or try and pick my way through the briars. I would have preferred a few more options, but having none, I made the only sensible decision and began climbing up the bank. I quickly realized it was impossible to pick one's way through a briar patch in the dark and by the time I finally escaped the patch of thorny little brambles I felt like I'd been in a knife fight with the Jets and Sharks and was the only one without a knife. I was cut to shreds. I headed toward what appeared to be a streetlight I estimated to be two to three hundred yards away. Just when I began to think I was going to reach the light without doing further damage to my body I tripped on a railroad track, skinning both knees and elbows. I lay on the tracks until I ran out of curse words, then got to my feet and stumbled on up the hill through another briar patch.

When I finally reached a street paralleling the railroad tracks I realized that what had, at a distance, appeared to be a streetlight flickering through the trees was a light attached to the underside of a breezeway between a house and a detached garage sitting on the upside of the street. Except for the single outside light the house was dark. A house farther up the street had light streaming from every window, two cars were parked in the driveway, and I could see people moving around inside the house. I surmised the family in the first house had left for the holiday weekend, visiting with friends or relatives, while just the reverse was happening at their neighbor's house with family or friends visiting them for the weekend. I hoped I was right because the breeze had turned my leotards, tights, and long underwear into an air-conditioning evaporator coil and I was beginning to shiver and my teeth were actually chattering. Hoped I was right! Hell, I had to be right or I was either going to freeze to death, get arrested for breaking and entering, or perhaps even get shot. The way my luck was running it would most likely be all three.

I tried the door on the side of the garage next to the house and to my amazement it opened. Either people in the neighborhood were very trusting or in their haste to get on the road the family forgot to lock the door. I didn't care either way, I was due a change of luck, but I figured to make up for this bit of good fortune a Doberman pinscher would be waiting for me inside the garage. Again, I didn't care one way or another—my only concern was to get out of my wet clothes and find some way to get my body heat back to normal before I died of hypothermia.

I entered the garage, closed the door behind me and fumbled around on the wall until I found a light switch, I flipped the switch and was blinded momentarily as light flooded the garage. A pickup truck stood against the far wall, the empty space between me and the pickup, where I suspected the family car was normally parked, was a pretty fair indication no one was home—my newfound good luck seemed to be holding.

All sorts of things were stored on overhead shelves along three walls of the garage; I spotted a couple of old military sleeping bags shoved between an ice chest and a fishing tackle box. I used a garden rake to pull one of the down-filled bags off the shelf, then opened a door on the pickup, spread the mummy-style bag on the seat, pulled off what was left of my wet clothes, crawled inside the sleeping bag and pulled it up over my head. By now my shaking was uncontrollable; only sheer determination, fueled by my desire to live, enabled me to zip the bag shut.

I had barely settled into the bag and although I was still shaking uncontrollably and my teeth were chattering so bad I suspect they could have been heard outside the garage, I began feeling warmer, my eyelids became heavy and I wanted to go to sleep. I didn't know if it was a myth or not, but I'd always heard you started feeling warm and got sleepy just before freezing to death. I tried to stay awake by thinking about all the good times, like growing up in West Texas, biking with my old navy buddies and of course, Candi. I remembered the first time I saw her and the way she made me feel, pictured her surfing naked in the warm waters of Baja and recalled every curve of her gorgeous body.

It is impossible to know at what point the reality of my conscious recollection of favorite memories became the dreams of my secret passions. I only know when the shadowy images faded and I began to clear away the cobwebs from my mind I realized I was alive. I didn't know how long I had slept, but when I unzipped the sleeping bag and stuck my head out, daylight was flooding the garage through a rear window. For a moment or two I was puzzled by my surroundings, but everything came back in a rush and I sat up abruptly, bumping my head against the top of the pickup, which drew another string of curses.

As I crawled out of the sleeping bag I became aware of several things all at once—I was naked, my right shoulder was sore, every joint was stiff, and as a result of wading through the briars my entire body was a mess of bloody scabs. I slipped on a pair of coveralls I found behind the truck seat and limped toward the door.

I cracked open the door a few inches and stood several minutes, watching and listening. Hearing nothing and seeing nothing I moved quickly across the space of 10 feet to the house, climbed two steps onto a back porch and checked the door; it was locked. I felt above the door frame in hopes of finding a key, but found nothing. I looked underneath the doormat and came up empty. I checked a nearby flowerpot with the same results. I walked back down the steps and over to a redwood picnic table, knelt down, looked underneath the table and smiled. A key was hanging on a hook screw attached to the underside of the table.

I opened the door slowly, slipped inside and closed the door without making a sound, then stood motionless for several seconds without hearing anything except the nearby refrigerator motor and a leaky faucet somewhere in another part of the house. I was relatively confident nobody was home, but I made a cursory walk through the house just to make sure, and then returned to the kitchen.

The fat burgers I'd eaten at the greasy spoon the day before were the last food I'd had and my stomach was beginning to think my throat had been cut, so with the house all to myself the only thing on my mind at the moment was food. I would decide how to get out of my predicament later. The refrigerator yielded lots of leftover goodies and my appetite was soon satiated. Now, it was time to come up with a plan. I needed clothes, money, and transportation, but first I wanted to take a nice long soak in a hot bath.

It was fairly evident from all the bath fragrances in the master bathroom that someone in the house preferred baths to showers. I opened the hot-water tap in the large tub and dumped in a handful of perfumed milk bath crystals from an apothecary jar sitting on the vanity and poured in a quarter bottle of bubble bath. While the tub filled I looked through the medicine cabinet and found a pair of tweezers and a bottle of iodine. The hot water stung my skinned knees and elbows, the briar scratches were even more sensitive to the hot water as several thorns had broken off and were still in some of the deeper cuts, but this was offset by the soothing effect the hot soapy water had on my stiff joints and aching muscles. I used the tweezers to remove the thorns and after about half an hour, when the water no longer felt hot, I got out of the tub, dried off and treated my scrapes and cuts with the iodine. Although the wound inflicted by the rock before I exited the river wasn't bleeding, it looked pretty nasty. I gritted my teeth, poured some iodine into the gash and, using gauze and tape from the medicine cabinet, wrapped it tight enough to pull the edges together.

I slipped on a bathrobe from the bedroom closet and returned to the kitchen, removed a beer from the refrigerator, walked into the living room, picked up the TV remote, turned on the television and eased myself down into a recliner opposite the TV set. It was the wrong time of day to get any news, so I watched Nebraska beat Oklahoma in a game that went back and forth until the Cornhuskers pulled it out in the last few minutes of the game.

When the evening news finally came on I was surprised to learn the authorities were launching such an extensive search in the exact area where I had intended to jump. I figured the crew had been alerted by some type of warning device when I released the rear stairs and surmised I had jumped a minute or two later. The search, however, was going to be called off until morning due to bad weather. Since I could say with absolute certainly they weren't going to turn up anything in the area they were searching, I knew there was a possibility the FBI would decide to expand their search another 25 miles all the way to the Oregon border, in which case I didn't want to be walking around without identification or any visible means of support; my wallet had floated away with my trousers. I figured I had better stay put for another night.

I suspected Candi had been staying on top of the news and was mystified when the airline stated the hijacker got away with two hundred thousand dollars. I decided, since I didn't have the money, there was no need for Candi to ever know there really was only two hundred thousand dollars and not the two million she thought she was getting. I would dispute their claim that I asked for only two hundred thousand dollars and argue the airline executives were playing head games. Since they didn't have the note to back their claims, I figured I could convince her Northwest Orient didn't want any would-be hijackers to know I actually got away with two million dollars so as not to encourage the next hijacker to up the ante—no doubt there would be copycats. I reasoned Candi would be upset enough with me for losing what she thought was two million dollars, but would consider it a double-cross and be twice as upset if I admitted asking for only two hundred thousand. I was afraid she just might be upset enough to turn me in if a reward were posted.

I knew the folks living in the house would be home sooner or later—hopefully it would be later and I would be long gone—but I knew I shouldn't take any chances and decided to leave the next day. I hit the refrigerator again. I didn't know when or where I would find my next meal, and the owners could come home at any time, in which case I would be leaving in a hurry. I figured I might as well depart with a full stomach. I cleaned up the kitchen and put everything back the way I'd found it, then checked around for something to wear. I took a pair of Levis, a flannel shirt and a windbreaker from an area in the back of the bedroom closet; I figured stuff in back was less likely to be missed. An old pair of brogans sitting on the floor in the hall closet and a pair of wool socks from a bureau drawer completed my get-away outfit. I was pleasantly surprised when everything fit fairly well. The boots were a little big, but what the hell, they were free.

I took the coveralls back to the garage and stuck them behind the seat in the truck where I'd found them, picked up the clothes I'd stripped off before crawling into the sleeping bag and hid them underneath the trash in a 30-gallon garbage can by the door. After putting the sleeping bag back on the shelf, I put the garden rake back where I'd found it and returned to the house.

Getting across the bridge to Portland by either a taxi or bus was going to require money; my other choice was to steal a car. I was tempted to take the pickup in the garage, but figured it might alert the authorities to the fact that they were searching 25 miles too far to the north. A jewelry box in the bedroom had two twenty-dollar bills and some change in one of the drawers; I took one twenty and left the other along with the change. There were several rings, gold chains and earrings in the top tray of the box. I don't know why, but I was attracted to an inconspicuous-looking gold ring with a solitaire red stone and what appeared to be a matching gold band with five smaller red stones. I pocketed the rings and was tempted to take more, but I knew if I took several pieces they would more than likely be missed right away. I was counting on the two rings not being missed for a long time and even then I was hoping the owner might think she had misplaced them. In another bedroom with stuffed animals on the bed and posters of rock stars on the wall I found a glass frog half full of change. I removed the stopper from the frog's underside and shook out the contents onto the bed. I took ten dollars in quarters and half dollars then put the rest of the change back inside the frog and returned him to his previous resting place on the floor by the door.

I went through the house making sure everything was exactly as I'd found it; unless someone questioned the missing food, clothing, or money right away they might never realize the hijacker had spent a couple on nights in their home. I remained fully dressed, anticipating the worst, and slept on the couch. I didn't sleep well. I awoke several times to imagined noises as well as real ones and each time had trouble going back to sleep. Five minutes later I would be awake again. When I finally did fall into a sound sleep I slept way past sunup.

I raided the refrigerator one last time, checked outside to make sure no one was wandering around the yard or walking down the street or driveway, then slipped out the back, locked the door and replaced the key on the hook underneath the picnic table where I'd found it, walked down the driveway to the street and turned west.

Following streets paralleling the river I crossed underneath Interstate 5 and into the heart of Vancouver about two hours later. During the walk into town I'd had time to rethink my problem of getting across the river and decided I should stay clear of the bus station. I reasoned that composite drawings were out by now and one would be posted at the ticket window where bus station employees could easily make comparisons to anyone buying tickets. I located a pawnshop and hung around outside until a guy drove up and went inside with stuff to pawn. I waited about fifteen seconds and then entered the store and walked up to the counter, where a guy I assumed to be the owner was looking over an impact wrench and a belt sander. I pretended to be interested in one of the watches in the showcase underneath the counter. When the pawnbroker announced he could let the guy have ten dollars on the power sander and fifteen dollars on the impact wrench the guy grimaced, bit his lip, hesitated for a few seconds, then agreed to what the pawnbroker offered.

While the required paperwork was being filled out, I went outside and waited by the guy's car. I figured if he needed money bad enough to pawn two hundred dollars' worth of stuff for twenty-five bucks he would be more than willing to take me across the bridge for a quick twenty dollars. I was right. He let me off a couple of blocks from the hotel where Candi was anxiously waiting for me to arrive with her money. Ten minutes later I walked into the hotel, up the stairs, knocked on the door and waited to deliver the bad news and face the music. It wasn't going to be pretty.

Candi opened the door, grabbed me, pulled me inside the room and smothered me with kisses. When she realized I wasn't carrying the money pouch she pushed me away and asked in a panicked voice, "Where's the money?"

"I lost it." Her voice went up about two octaves and she screeched,

"You what?"

"I lost it in the river. I came down in the river less than 10 miles from here. The parachute and harness sank with the money still attached." She looked at me for several seconds, her eyes wide with disbelief, then her face hardened, her eyes narrowed to mere slits, and she hissed, "You're lying."

"No, I'm not." She threw herself at me, flailing away at my face with her fists. I grabbed her hands and held her at arm's length. She struggled for a moment or two, then tried to bite my hand. When I jerked my hand away she kicked me in the groin. I slapped her hard across the face and threw her onto the bed. She didn't come at me again, she just sat on the bed glaring at me.

"You're lying. You hid the money, you're going to dump me and keep all the money for yourself."

"If my intentions were to dump you and keep all the money for myself, why would I be here now? Why would I have bothered coming back just to tell you I lost the money and then leave without you?" She thought about what I had said for a few seconds.

"I don't know. Maybe you are going to kill me so there won't be anyone around who knows you did it."

"If I were going to kill you, why wouldn't I have brought the money with me and killed you at a time when you wouldn't be expecting anything?" My argument was beginning to have an effect on her. She continued to sit on the bed just staring at me. After several seconds, in a calmer voice she said, "You're joking, this is just one of your sick jokes, right?"

"Look at me, do these clothes look familiar?" I ripped off the shirt and windbreaker, then removed the Levis to expose the cuts and scratches and my skinned knees and elbows. She didn't say anything, but kept looking at me as though she didn't believe a word I was saying. I told her everything, starting with not being able to locate any landmarks, getting knocked off the stairs, coming down in the river, told her how I would have died of hypothermia had I not been lucky enough to find a house with nobody home and about getting back across the river to Portland.

"Why didn't you ask for two million like we agreed? They said you only asked for two hundred thousand dollars." Apparently she believed my story and was now just trying to pick a fight. Well, it was time to sell the lie or I would never hear the end of it.

"What?" I asked. It was my turn to disbelieve what I was hearing or pretend to anyway.

"You heard me, you didn't get two million—they only gave you two hundred thousand." I kept up the act.

"What are you talking about?"

"It's all over the news. They said you asked for two hundred thousand dollars and that's what they gave you. And besides that, they know you did it! How could you be so stupid as to buy the ticket in your own name?" Now I truly was in disbelief of what I was hearing.

"Are you crazy?" She reached over, picked up a newspaper from the nightstand, shoved it in my face, and sneered, "See for yourself."

I read the part about the FBI agent saying the hijacker had bought a ticket in the name of D. B. Cooper and blurted out, "They're lying." I went into the story about the airlines not wanting future hijackers to think they would pay two million dollars, but I was dumbfounded and without an answer as to how they knew D. B. Cooper was the hijacker.

"I swear to you I did not once use the name D. B. Cooper and there was two million dollars." I admitted I almost blew it, relating how, with my mind on other things, I answered Cooper when the ticket agent asked my name, but regained my senses in time and gave him the name Dan. Dan Cooper. I suspected there must be a real person named D. B. Cooper, but I couldn't tell Candi because she believed my name was D. B. Cooper—what a tangled web we weave when first we practice to deceive. It was sometime later that we learned a reporter searching through police records had discovered the name D. B. Cooper. The only thing I can figure is the police turned in a report after coming to the motel to investigate the disturbance called in by the night manager when the special forces guy almost killed me because Candi and I tried to run the badger game on him.

Once Candi accepted the fact that I had lost the money, I didn't have much trouble convincing her the powers that be at Northwest Orient were scamming the public about the actual amount of money I'd gotten away with.

Except to eat, we stayed in our room until the day our flight left for Hawaii. Days passed so slowly they seemed like weeks. We watched TV rather than talk and chance arguing. While we waited, the emotional firestorm I endured when I arrived without the money subsided. I knew it would surface again. It was just a matter of time.

Although Candi was still ice cold when our departure date finally arrived, the ride to the airport was uneventful and we boarded the airplane without anyone giving us a second glance.

The Islands

The sun was hanging just above the horizon when our plane slipped past Diamond Head and Waikiki before touching down at Honolulu International. As we entered the terminal, the many pleasures and memorable experiences from my navy days came flooding back as the soft strains of Hawaiian ukuleles reached my ears. A threesome were strumming ukuleles and singing "Aloha Oe" while two lovely Polynesian ladies danced the hula, and two other young Polynesian ladies slipped leis over the heads of arriving tourists. Hawaii is a place where people go to discard identities, forget about their problems, and regenerate their energy. It was working for me. I had already forgotten about Candi's tantrums and the fact that I had let two hundred thousand dollars slip through my fingers and almost died in the Columbia River. I was remembering evenings at Pearl City Tavern, nights on Hotel Street, and midnight swims on moonlit beaches where I acted out my own *From Here to Eternity* fantasies with various local girls.

The driver wouldn't let us on the bus with our luggage so I laid out ten bucks for a taxi to Waikiki. We checked into a hotel on Lewers Street, left our stuff in the room, kicked off our shoes, and headed for the beach. By then only the hint of a sunset remained on the horizon as the day gave way to the night. Plumeria and night-blooming jasmine wafted on the evening trades, and the sound of distant ukuleles and Hawaiian guitars beckoned to us from hotel lanais, where luaus were getting underway beneath flickering tiki torches. Apparently, I wasn't the only one overcome by the Island ambience—Candi no longer made a display of her disappointment or showed any hostility toward me for not keeping my promise to make her rich. As we walked along the sand with gentle waves rolling up the beach to bathe our feet in warm tropical water and swirling white foam, Candi slipped her hand in mine, moved close, and laid her head on my shoulder. Neither of us made a subsequent show of affection until, after walking in silence for several minutes, Candi let go of my hand and ran into the surf. I raced after her, catching up as she attempted to dive over an incoming breaker, but the wave knocked us off our feet and rolled us back onto the beach where it deposited us in a tangled heap. When she threw her arms around me and I saw the sparkle in her eyes and that devilish smile on her lips I knew all was forgiven, at least for the moment.

We left trails of water as we walked through the hotel lobby, but no one paid much attention to us even though it was obvious to the most casual observer that Candi was naked underneath her wet sundress. It was no big deal; they'd seen it all before.

We barely entered the room and I had yet to close the door when Candi's wet sundress hit the floor, I ripped off my soggy clothes and raced her to the bed. Things were back to normal. It was hours later before we started thinking or talking about food even though, except for snacks the airline provided, we hadn't eaten since early morning. We showered, got dressed and headed for Trader Vic's in the International Market Place—a restaurant famous for creating the mai tai. Neither of us mentioned our failed get-rich scheme. We ate and talked about things to come, pretty much like we had done in the topless joint in South Tacoma where we first met and where fate, without the benefit of ceremony, had joined us together for better or for worse, and I suspected, until death intervened. Adversity was no stranger to either of us—we had grown all too familiar with the heartaches of failure and we knew we had to let it go. Time heals all wounds or so they say. I don't know about that, but perhaps here in paradise we would find it easier to live with our disappointment and eventually it might even fade from our memory.

The mai tai was a combination of different types of rum, curaçao, orgret, ginger, lime, and pineapple that went down smooth and easy and left you wanting another, but it was so potent Trader Vic's limited you to only two at any one sitting, or so they said. I managed to finagle a third round by denying we had our first while waiting for dinner to arrive. I don't know how we got back to our room—all I remember is a lot of touching and giggling as we made our way along Kalakaua Avenue. I also remember people stopping to watch us as we passed. I've often wondered what we did to cause people to turn their heads and watch us. I don't even remember arriving back at the hotel, much less what we did along the way, but knowing Candi as I did, I imagine we put on quite a show.

The next morning when Candi woke me the way she had so many times before when her spirits were flying high, I knew the bad times were behind us and I was going to enjoy living in paradise. It was almost noon before we left the room and walked down to the Royal Hawaiian for brunch. The Royal Hawaiian was too expensive for us to make it a habit, but since Candi had accepted the fact she wasn't going to be rich anytime in the near future and hadn't brought up the subject since we left the hotel room in Portland, I decided to treat her to a taste of the living she had dreamed about while helping me plan Operation Quick Rich. That evening I took her to Willows, where we ate shrimp curry, drank jasmine tea and tossed food from our plates to koi swimming in pools underneath our table.

The following morning we went to the Moana and ate breakfast on the lanai underneath the old banyan tree where the radio program "Hawaii Calls" originated, and made plans for the rest of the day. Candi rented a surfboard from a concessionaire on the beach behind the police station and took to the waves while I looked through the Honolulu Advertiser for a car to purchase. After a few phone calls I found a sailor at Barbers Point who was PCSing and agreed to sell me a '64 Chevy Malibu rag-top for six hundred dollars, and said he would meet me at my hotel that evening after he got off duty. When I saw the car I realized why he had jumped at my offer. Mechanically, the Chevy was fairly sound, but the body had more rust than paint and the top was held together with duct tape. Nevertheless, Candi loved it, so I forked over the money, he signed the title, and we were all happy with the transaction.

That evening I was still in my be-nice-to-Candi mode and took her to the Kahala Hilton, where we dined outside on a terrace overlooking the ocean. I watched Candi as she sat bathed in moonlight and it was easy to see, by the way she delicately touched the linen napkin to her lips before lifting the tall, stemmed glass to sip her wine, and by how natural her movements were with the fork she held so daintily, that this was a lifestyle to which she had been born. There was no way I could possibly know how much she missed the life she had known growing up in La Jolla and as I listened to the enchanting sounds of The Islands and breathed in the subtle fragrances of the night, I wished more than anything I could give her back the life she had thrown away but secretly still wanted even though she pretended it didn't matter, and silently cursed myself for losing the money.

Candi must have been reading my thoughts and maybe even felt my pain. She reached across the table, put her hand on mine, gave it a little squeeze, flashed me a smile I had never seen before, and whispered, "Forget about it, it's okay."

She looked up and made a sweeping gesture with her hand. "I don't need all this, really it's okay. Tomorrow let's find a place to live where we'll fit in and forget about what was never meant to be." That was a side of Candi I had never seen before and I wondered if perhaps she cared for me more than I realized.

Early the next morning we put the top down on the Malibu, which Candi had affectionately christened the Rusty Bucket—a word play on the California custom cars of the '50s known as buckets—and drove up to Haleiwa on the north shore, where I bought Candi a used surfboard and a new bikini. Candi was eager to try the new board so we stopped at Waimea. The big surf hadn't arrived on north Oahu yet, but there were enough good waves for Candi to show her stuff. After a half dozen sets the usual crowd had gathered to watch and, no doubt, wonder who is this thirty-year-old *haole* girl who made the Duke (Kahanomokou) look like an amateur.

After a couple of hours Candi stuck her board in the back seat of the Malibu, and we drove over to Sunset Beach. The waves weren't as good as they were at Waimea, so we drove on around the North Shore and down the windward side. We stopped for lunch at Haiku Gardens in Kaneohe, a place introduced to me by a girl in Kahaluu during my navy days. After lunch we continued our around-the-island tour, taking the tourist route to reacquaint ourselves with Oahu. It had been more than ten years since either of us had been to Hawaii. I had been stationed at Pearl Harbor; Candi vacationed with her parents. We stopped at Sandy Beach, but the waves were breaking too close to shore for Candi's liking. The blowhole wasn't active and we weren't in the mood for snorkeling, so we passed up Hanauma Bay. Before driving back into Waikiki we stopped at the pullout just above the Kupikpikio Point lighthouse, sat on the rock wall above the cliffs, and watched the sun set while feeding potato chips to a couple of cats hiding in the underbrush below the wall. In the distance a handful of surfers were trying to catch a few waves before nightfall.

It was time to get serious about finding a place to live, so on the way to our room I picked up a newspaper someone had left in the hotel lobby.

When I began perusing the news section, a newly acquired habit, checking to see if there were any new leads on D. B. Cooper, I had a hard time containing myself. I gave Candi one of those cat-ate-the-canary smiles and showed her a picture of a girl wearing a T-shirt with a big bundle of money attached to a parachute and an airplane flying away in the distance. The T-shirt asked the question, "D. B. Cooper, where are you?"

When Candi saw the picture her eyes got real big, but before she could say anything I asked, "Wouldn't they like to know?"

She cracked a big smile and said, "You're famous. You're going to go down in history with all the other people who did things no one ever did before. You'll be listed with people like Lindbergh, Sir Hillary, and even Columbus. How does it feel to be famous?"

"Well, I don't know. I haven't thought about it, but I can truthfully say I'd rather be rich than famous. I just can't get over it, our plan worked perfectly until I came down in the middle of the Columbia River. I think God hates us both." Candi was no longer smiling when she replied,

"Yeah, maybe so, but look at the bright side. We're here in Hawaii, which is a lot better than jail or cold, wet, smelly Tacoma, so let's forget about it."

"I know, but we worked damn hard for that money. It's ours, we earned it."

"Hey, get over it. Come on, show some class." She seemed to be having a good time harassing me, but I was afraid she was suppressing her disappointment and perhaps even anger that was going to come back to haunt me some day in a very unpleasant way.

Candi looked at the picture again and after reading the accompanying article announced, in a voice tinged with envy and perhaps a bit of animosity, "Some guy made a hundred and eighty dollars selling these T-shirts in just two days. We should go into business selling D. B. Cooper products."

"Well, first of all, we don't want to attract any unnecessary attention and second, you need money to go into business. I lost our money, remember?" Candi seemed a little upset with me when she said, "I told you to forget about the money." She was silent for several seconds than excitedly blurted out, "You should write a book about how you did it. With all the speculation about D. B. Cooper circulating in newspapers and on television everybody would buy a book written by the real D. B. Cooper."

"Yeah, well, maybe one day after the statute of limitations expires."

"Now is the time! Haven't you heard the saying, 'Strike while the iron is hot'?"

"Yeah, but how am I going to spend the money if I'm in jail?"

"Oh, don't worry about that, I'll spend it for you."

"I bet you would, wouldn't you?" She gave me one of her devilish little smiles and answered, "Sure I would."

We agreed, for different reasons, the north shore was the best place to live. Candi had surf and sun in mind while I figured the authorities wouldn't be looking on Oahu's north shore for a guy who jumped out of an airplane in a business suit with a bag full of money. Actually, I wasn't all that concerned, there were so many people hijacking airplanes at gunpoint these days I figured the Feds didn't give much thought to me. I mean it was so bad the airlines were paying federal agents (sky marshals) to ride on their airplanes. When you looked at it logically, I didn't have a gun, didn't hurt anybody, only got away with two hundred thousand dollars—hell, I wasn't worth the time and money it would take to catch me. And to make things more interesting and a headache for federal agents, the counterculture had turned me into a hero. The guy on the street was pulling for me to get away and never be caught; people were even wearing T-shirts with my name on them. So it was unlikely anyone who might have been able to help the Feds would volunteer any information. And if the truth be known, I was willing to bet the authorities still hadn't figured out what to charge me with even if they caught me. In another year my file would probably get tossed in with the rest of the unsolved cases, never to be revisited. I found myself smiling. Hell, they'd probably already given up.

Haleiwa was mostly a mixed bag of leftover hippies, beach bums, hanger-on flower children, and dopeheads. *Paco lolo* (crazy weed) and incense, not plumeria and jasmine were the dominant aromas of the north shore. Candi and I pretended to be from Pacific Beach, a suburb of San Diego which we both knew well—knowing the area was important in case we met up with someone from southern California with a lot of questions—and we blended in without a hitch. Within a couple of weeks I knew the social structure of the community, who to see to get what as well as who not to ask. I knew the power brokers as well as the snitches. This was all very important since I needed to figure out a way to keep a little jingle in my pocket.

When the big waves arrived Candi was on her board almost every day. She had planned to pick up some prize money when the surfing contests got underway, but gave up the idea when a television crew showed up at Sunset Beach for the first heat of the first contest she entered—besides her parents and perhaps the authorities back in Denver, I wondered who might be looking for her.

As my money began to run low I turned to the only trade at which I considered myself to be an expert, pot farming. I let the word out I was an experienced grower from California looking for a partner to finance me. I hooked up with a couple of locals, two brothers from Waimanalo, who had tried their hand at pot farming for the first time the previous summer but had barely broken even, and who were looking for a partner who knew the trade. We were made for each other.

I began climbing high in the Koolau along the windward side and found Hawaii tailor made for marijuana farming. It had lots of small out-of-the-way valleys with plenty of sun and rain, accessible only on foot with great difficulty. I found a couple of well-hidden lava tubes with good water, which I converted into makeshift hothouses. It took a couple of dozen trips to get enough black plastic sheeting, insulation, 12-volt light fixtures, a 100 feet of PVC, plus a couple of heavy-duty automotive alternators and a lot of other equipment up to the lava tubes, but when I finished I had enough stuff to build two insulated enclosures inside the lava tubes with plenty of hydroelectric power to warm the plant beds and grow lights when the seed sprouted.

By using the hothouses we had plants ready to transplant into ideal growing areas before other growers planted seed. This gave us the advantage of harvesting earlier. We had our paco lolo down the mountain and sold before other farmers had cut their first plant and weeks before government agents started watching for activity on the trails used by growers to get their crops to market. The return on my associates' investment was better than a hundred to one—needless to say, they were quite happy. As a matter of fact, they were so happy they made me a full partner and gave me a third of the profit.

I never thought it would happen, but shortly after I got my share of the money from our marijuana crop, Candi announced she had had enough surf and sun for a while and was ready for a change of scenery. I think she was more tired of living in a tent on the beach and using public toilets and showers than she was of surf and sun—money had been almost nonexistent the last couple of months before our crop sold. When I suggested we get a Winnebago and travel about the country for a while Candi quickly agreed—at that time Winnebago was synonymous with *motor home* in many segments of society, and that remains true even today in some circles.

The big jet swooped low over Balboa Park and settled down in the heart of the city. It was early morning—flights bound for the mainland always seemed to leave Honolulu late at night—and the sun was climbing into a clear blue southern California sky. For a moment my thoughts returned to a time almost twenty years past when, as a navy recruit, I stepped off the train and thought San Diego, with its green hills and blue water, must be the most beautiful place on earth.

Although Candi hadn't complained, I knew she was more than ready for something a little more comfortable than a tent on the beach. I figured I would try and make it up to her for the way the lack of funds had forced her to live for the last couple of months, and give her a few days in a luxury hotel. When we arrived at Lindbergh Field I tried to rent a car, but without a credit card, none of the agencies wanted to rent me a vehicle even though I was willing to put up a cash deposit, so we took a taxi to Shelter Island and checked into the Half Moon Inn.

Candi wanted to eat at several upscale restaurants she remembered. Most required a coat and tie for me and a dress for her. A taxi dropped us at a shopping center in Mission Valley, where Candi bought a couple of minidresses and all sorts of accessories. When I asked why a dress or handbag cost so much she answered, "Oh, it's Yves St. Laurent," or "It's Chanel," as though the mere mention of a name explained everything. So began my education in designer clothing and accessories.

Whoever designed the minidress had Candi in mind. With her long legs, slender body, and curves in all the right places she was a knockout in a minidress. She turned heads wherever we went. At first I was afraid she would attract the attention of some law enforcement type who might take a second look at her escort and connect me with the composite drawing of D. B. Cooper, even though it wasn't a good likeness, but after further consideration I figured if they were looking at her they wouldn't be looking at me. Candi tried to talk me into buying some "mod" clothes—it wasn't my thing. I bought a navy blazer, khaki pants, a couple of light blue shirts with white button-down collars, a burgundy tie and a pair of wingtips. Even then I felt out of place; denim and cowboy boots were my thing.

A month in San Diego cost us almost six grand, which was more money than we'd had when we arrived in Hawaii and ten times the amount we had lived on for the last couple of months prior to selling our crop, but what the hell—easy come, easy go. For a declared socialist, Candi sure had expensive tastes. We ate at the Star of the Sea—I loved their abalone—Lubach's, Mister A's, Top of the Cove, and some

I can't remember. All were great restaurants but I liked Lubach's best—they had great beef stroganoff. Mister A's had the best view of any restaurant we visited; their steak Diane wasn't bad either. I don't know if it was being back in San Diego, having new and fashionable clothes to wear, having money to spend after just getting by for so long, or trying to reacquaint herself with the lifestyle she'd left behind when she ran away from home—whatever the reason, Candi was a different person. Not only did she want to eat in gourmet restaurants every night, she wanted entertainment as well. We started out going to a movie and dancing afterwards—she sure liked dancing, we danced almost every night. But going to a movie wasn't enough, we went to concerts at the civic center, and theater at the Old Globe. We even took in a Chargers' game, which was more to my liking. My taste in entertainment wasn't as refined as Candi's; however, the exposure to a more eloquent and cultured lifestyle was having its effect.

The places I had frequented around San Diego during my navy days were far less sophisticated than the ones I experienced with Candi. Nevertheless, I would have liked to revisit several of them, but I didn't want to hang around too long and chance running into someone I knew—I could only imagine what might happen should Candi hear an acquaintance from my past address me by my real name—so I cast aside nostalgia and decided against taking in any of my old haunts.

I figured we had hung around San Diego long enough and it was time to get on with our plans of traveling about the country in a Winnebago before anything unpleasant turned up, so I bought a copy of the *San Diego Union* and began scrutinizing the advertisements for a used motor home.

When looking to buy a used item, there are several good reasons to check out the military community first. Military people often receive overseas assignments without prior warning, which requires selling cars, recreational vehicles, stereo equipment, and household goods at short notice at a price usually below market, and service people in general answer honestly about why they're selling and are up front about any existing problems. San Diego, being a navy town, made it easy to find exactly what I was looking for—a sailor shipping out and desperate to sell an almost new motor home. The advertisement read, "Nothing down, take over payments on one-year-old motor home." The owner said he would meet us, around noon, at Bank of America on Eighth Street in National City, where the motor home was being financed and the title was being held.

About ten thirty the next morning we checked out of our room at the Half Moon Inn, left our bags with the bellman and took a taxi to National City. The driver dropped us in front of a Mexican restaurant I remembered from the time I was stationed at the Thirty-second Street naval station and lived in National City with my Filipino wife. The restaurant, famous locally for creating the chimichanga, was anything but fancy. The food was a long way from Tex-Mex and not as good as I remembered—everything always seems better looking back—but it was still pretty good. After lunch we walked to the bank; a navy man in dress blues was already waiting inside and anxiously watching the door. I guess I had given him a fairly accurate description of what we looked liked because he headed straight for us the minute we entered the bank.

The motor home looked barely used. I gave it a casual once-over while the sailor instructed Candi on the proper operation of all the gadgets. Back inside the bank Candi surprised the young petty officer, as well as the bank manager, when she opened her purse and counted out sixty-eight one-hundred-dollar bills—Candi loved having, touching, counting, and yes, spending money. I think she was a socialist only when she didn't have access to money. The bank manager recounted the money and gave Candi some change. He then passed the title to the sailor who promptly signed it and handed it back to the bank manager, who in turned signed it and passed it over to Candi. We all shook hands, thanked one another, and went our separate ways.

As we drove along National Avenue, I was tempted to pull into the Westerner's parking lot, but not wanting to tempt fate passed on by without even a glance to that side of the street. I had spent too many nights at the Westerner, it was even money someone would remember me. For all I knew my ex-wife was still working there and I sure didn't want to open up that can of worms with Candi present. Had I been alone, I probably would have stopped.

I drove back to the Half moon Inn, picked up our bags from the bellman and headed back down Harbor Drive. At the Pacific Coast Highway I turned left, figuring I would cruise lower Broadway before cutting back over to G Street to pick up Highway 94. Nothing had changed much on the west end of Broadway—all the bars, tattoo parlors, bail bondsmen, and pawn shops still seemed to be in business. As I passed the Seven Seas Locker Club my mind flashed back to the incident probably responsible for starting me down the road I was now traveling and, in all likelihood, would continue traveling to an unpleasant terminus. I'd had a year in prison to reflect on my decision to appropriate the Harley without ever coming to a conclusion. I knew the answer, of course. It had been a spur-of-the-moment exercise in stupidity, but it is difficult to take credit for our own mistakes, so I wrote it off to one of those meant-to-happen things over which we have no control. It was the way I had come to look at life. I figured I was just passing through to some predestined end with no way to affect the outcome.

The motor home's gas gauge was bouncing on empty, so at College Avenue I exited Highway 94 onto Broadway in Lemon Grove, pulled into a Union 76 station and pumped 35 gallons into the Winnebago's gas tank. With the way gasoline prices were going up I was hoping I wouldn't need to fill the tank very often, which, as it turned out, wasn't the case, since the motor home got only between 7 and 8 miles to a gallon. I had to start looking for a gas station about every 250 miles. I parked in a supermarket parking lot where we loaded up on groceries, and then walked to a nearby Western wear and feed store where I bought a pair of new Justins, three shirts, a couple of pairs of Levis, a Stetson, and a new leather belt. Anytime there was any spending of money Candi made sure she spent her share. She matched me item for item and then some.

I got back onto Highway 94 at Massachusetts Avenue. By now we were both excited at the idea of living on the road. I recalled the times when I traveled about with my biker buddies, but this was a big step up from living out of a sea bag and sleeping on the ground. For Candi it brought back memories of backpacking the Redwood Highway during her flower child days. As I look back, it may have been the best time Candi and I ever spent together, but all good things come to an end sooner or later or so they say. In our case it seemed to be sooner rather than later. In a little over four months we were broke.

We learned about RVing by watching and talking with other RVers, staying mostly in state or federal parks; in the West we stayed on BLM land. By the end of January we decided to give up the out-of-the-way places and take in the Mardi Gras. We were fortunate to get a space at a commercial campground. The manager had just told us that all camper parks within a 100 miles of New Orleans were reserved months in advance during Mardi Gras. We were about to leave when the telephone rang. After talking briefly with whoever called, the manager hung up the phone and said, "You're in luck, I have a cancellation."

The camper park ran a shuttle four times a day to Jackson Square in the French Quarter. Most days Candi and I took the last bus leaving the camper park, stayed up all night, and caught the first bus back the following morning. We were partied out by the time Carnival wound to a close, which was just as well, because we were down to less than a hundred bucks. We had paid for a two-week stay in the camper park. With our money running out we figured it was a good time to catch up on our sleep and take a badly needed rest before getting on the road again. Actually, I figured it was time to head back to Hawaii and get my hotbeds planted. Candi agreed, so I put a For Sale sign in the window of the motor home.

It was then I noticed there were several other RVs with For Sale signs in their windows. Puzzled, I approached a foursome sitting at a table underneath the awning of a fifth-wheeler and started asking questions. I found that a lot of "fulltimers" (people who lived in their RVs full-time) were concerned about the future availability of gasoline due to recent action in Algeria, Iraq, and Libya, which were moving toward nationalizing the interests of foreign oil companies. Some leaders of Middle Eastern oil-producing countries had formed something called OPEC (Organization of Petroleum-Exporting Countries) and were talking about an alliance by which they would agree upon the amount of production, which in turn would control the price of a barrel of oil, laying the groundwork for not only expensive gasoline but shortages as well. It seemed a bit farfetched to me, but it was easy to see how it could happen. Since more than half of the world's known oil reserves were in the Middle East, if these oil-producing countries agreed on cutbacks in production they could, in a sense, hold the entire western world hostage.

When I asked their advice on how to sell the motor home and what I might be able to get for it, they started shaking their heads and asked what I paid. When I told them I paid sixty-eight hundred dollars there was more head shaking.

"You'll be lucky to get fifty cents on the dollar," one guy said. Another guy chimed in, "Thirty cents on the dollar is probably more realistic."

When I asked where I might be able to sell the motor home, there was a continuation of head shaking, and the first guy said the closest place was probably Baton Rouge. Another guy suggested I could probably get a better price in Houston. The logic was that with the probability of an oil shortage in the not too distant future, Texas was poised for a boom in the oil service industry, with new wells being drilled and old wells, which had been capped because of low production, would be reopened. Houston seemed to be the hub of all the new activity. I thanked them for the information and their advice and sauntered back to tell Candi what I'd learned.

I figured Candi would be stressed at the idea of losing three or four thousand dollars when we sold the motor home, providing we could find a buyer, and go into one of her, "all the things we could do with four thousand dollars" tantrums, but she didn't seem to care as long as we could get back to Hawaii.

I broke out the road atlas left in the rig by the previous owner, and calculated the distance to Houston at about 350 miles. We should still have a few dollars in our pockets when we arrived. With nothing to do, we got a good night's sleep and hit the road early enough the following morning to avoid rush-hour traffic.

We got into Houston about two that afternoon and stopped at the first RV sales lot we found. The salesman told us the owner wasn't buying RVs for the time being, citing the same concerns I'd heard at the RV park in New Orleans, but he knew a dealer who was buying just about anything if the price was right and asked if I wanted him to give the guy a call. I told him I'd appreciate any help he could give me. He got the guy on the line and described the motor home, telling him it looked to be in pretty good condition, and then asked if I had a clear title and how much I was looking to get for it. I told him the title was clear, but I hadn't thought about a price and asked him what he suggested, adding that I wanted to sell pretty bad. The salesman covered the mouthpiece, which was probably just for show—I suspect he was getting a finder's fee—and said, "I'd ask thirty-five hundred and if, as you say, you're pretty desperate to sell I'd take whatever he offers, because there aren't a lot of buyers out there at this time, the gas scare being what it is." I nodded.

"Thirty-five sounds okay to me." He removed his hand from the mouthpiece and said,

"He's looking for a quick sale, says he'd like to get about thirty-five hundred and says the title is clear." He paused for a couple of seconds, and then said, "Okay, I'll send him over." He hung up the phone, gave us instructions on how to find the RV sales lot and the name of the guy to see once we found the place.

This guy reminded me of the bottom feeders around military bases taking advantage of men in uniform who had fallen on hard times. He lowballed us at two grand. After a bit of haggling we agreed to twenty-five hundred dollars providing he paid in cash and called us a taxi. He became a bit suspicious after looking over the title Candi handed him and asked to see my driver's license. When the name on the title didn't match the name on my driver's license he asked several more questions—I knew he was thinking we were trying to pawn off a stolen vehicle on him. I explained since the sailor we purchased the motor home from reregistered it only one month before we bought it, I couldn't see any reason to change the title into my name since we would be selling it before time ran out on the current registration. He was still a bit skeptical, but a call to Bank of America in National City confirmed that the title was indeed clear, so he paid us in cash and called a taxi as agreed, and shortly thereafter we were on our way to the airport. While we waited for the taxi I asked him why he was buying RVs since so many people were concerned about the possibility of gas shortages as well as higher prices in the near future. He said he didn't believe there was going to be a shortage and even if there was it would last no more than a year, perhaps two years at the outside, and then everybody would be wanting RVs again. He would at least double his money within two or three years. Looking back, I guess he made a lot of money.

Returning to Paradise

Regardless of how long you have been off Island, ten days or ten years, when you deplane at Honolulu International the intermingling of sights, sounds, and aromas wipe away all memory between departure and return, leaving you with an unexplainable emotion, the feeling of having never left The Islands mixed with the same excitement you experienced on your first visit to paradise.

Not having fully recovered from two weeks of all-night partying at the Mardi Gras coupled with being broke and facing the prospect of not being able to sell the motor home had made our last couple of days on the road a bit trying, and we ended up fighting about things of little or no consequence. There was still a chill in the air when we boarded the plane in Houston and we remained silent for most of the long flight back to Oahu. Candi slept almost the entire flight after we changed planes in Los Angeles. I guess we both figured it was better not to talk than to argue.

When the Fasten Your Seat Belt sign came on and the captain announced we were making our approach into Honolulu I gently nudged Candi awake and informed her we were getting ready to land. She inhaled deeply and turned slightly toward me, presenting me with a profile of her shapely body as she held her hands behind her head stretching slowly from side to side with a slight twisting motion to work out the kinks. She was well aware I was watching her every move and no doubt knew what I was thinking. She fastened her seat belt and when she glanced at me there was the hint of the devilish little grin I had come to know so well. I sensed things between us would soon be back to normal. I was right.

As we strolled toward baggage claim to the soft strains of ukuleles, Candi moved close against me, and matched her stride to mine, and then took my hand in hers and gave it a little squeeze.

While we were waiting to make connections in Los Angeles, and unbeknown to Candi, I had called the hotel in Waikiki where we'd spent our first night in The Islands, and made reservations for three nights. We collected our bags and carted them to curbside where I motioned to the first taxi in line. We climbed into the back seat while the cabby loaded our bags into the trunk, and slipped in under the wheel. When I gave him the Lewers Street address Candi's head snapped around to face me, mischief was dancing in her eyes and the smile on her lips promised a very exciting evening.

The evening played out pretty much as it had on our first trip to paradise: a romp on the beach which ended up in the surf, a trail of water through the hotel lobby as we traipsed back to our room, a couple of hours on the bed, followed by a hot shower and dinner at Trader Vic's—only this time we complied with Trader Vic's two-Mai-Tai-maximum rule. The walk from Trader Vic's back to our hotel may not have been as exciting for tourists as it had been for the lucky passers-by we encountered on our first night in Waikiki, but for me, the events that followed—since this time I remembered everything that happened as the night unfolded—were even more thrilling.

The next morning we ate breakfast at the smorgasbord across the street from our hotel—if you're on a budget or just want an inexpensive meal, Perry's all-you-can-eat smorgasbord is the best deal on Oahu. After breakfast Candi and I went our separate ways. She bought a new bikini, rented a surfboard, and hit the waves. I made a call to my partners; it was time to get my plant beds started. My partners were excited to know I was back on Island and eager for me to get our growing operation started up again; we set up a meeting for later in the day at the Natatorium.

After the smiles, handshakes, and proper amount of small talk we got down to business. My partners still couldn't believe their good fortune in finding someone so knowledgeable of growing techniques. Neither could they believe how much money they had made with such a small investment. I hadn't contacted either of the brothers since I left Oahu and they feared I wasn't coming back. To make sure I stayed they agreed to a fifty/fifty split of the profits and to advance me ten thousand dollars for personal expenses and anther ten grand for supplies, providing I got started right away.

I was determined not to live in a tent on the beach, the way we had the year before, so I rented a one-bedroom condo on the beach at Punaluu. The windward Oahu location served a dual purpose; the mountains where I grew marijuana were practically across the road from the beach; the climb was not easy, but it gave me easy access to the area. The beach would keep Candi content and the big surf on the north shore was less than a half hour's drive.

Everything went well; we more than quadrupled our profit from the year before. My partners were ecstatic; so was Candi. She was eager to go back to the mainland and spend it all—I had other ideas. I still had the gold pesos I'd buried on my father's ranch back in Texas, but those coins were my rainy-day fund and I wouldn't cash them in except as a last resort.

Part of the deal I made with my partners precluded Candi from ever knowing how much money we made, neither was she to know about the cash advance which I deposited in two different banks in Kaneohe. It had become painfully clear to me that Candi would spend every penny she could get her hands on. I didn't want to spend like a drunken sailor for four or five months and be broke and just getting by for the rest of the year, so somewhere between our drive from New Orleans to Houston I decided to start putting some of my share of the profits into investments of some kind; I didn't want to grow *paco lolo* for the rest of my life. I didn't know anything about the stock market although I knew there was money to be made in stocks and bonds. I figured even if I never invested in the market it wouldn't hurt to have some idea about how it worked, so I bought a couple of books and started reading.

My source for books was a used bookstore in the basement of the library in Kaneohe. They had hundreds, if not thousands of books for sale and priced anywhere from ten cents to a dollar. I knew their books on investing were mostly outdated, but I figured the principle was pretty much the same whether written yesterday or a decade ago. A book on investing in real estate caught my eye. As I perused the first few pages the statement, "Real estate has created more millionaires than any other commodity," caught my eye. I purchased the book for a quarter; it was the best twenty-five cents I ever spent.

As it turned out, the secret, according to the author, was leveraging; by putting down a small amount of your own money and using the bank's money to make up the difference in the purchase price gave you the advantage of reaping all the benefits of increases due to appreciation and by renting out the property you would be letting the tenant make the mortgage payments and pay the real estate taxes. The author warned that there might be a negative cash flow in the early years due to vacancies and maintenance, but after a few years you would be putting money in your pocket because inflation would drive rents to higher levels.

Since we planted early we had a crop ready for market before most Island growers were considering their first harvest. I took a major portion of my share from the first sale and purchased a two-bedroom ocean side condominium at the Ilikai—I figured Waikiki property would appreciate faster than other parts of The Island. The rest of the money, except for the ten thousand, I gave to Candi who deposited it in the joint bank account we had opened the day after we returned to The Islands from Houston. I contracted with a local property management company to handle rentals, maintenance, taxes, and so forth—I set up an escrow account with enough money in it to cover mortgage payments for a year in case of unexpected problems. I insisted upon several things when contracting with the management company. They were a little apprehensive, but agreed when I insisted that under no circumstances would they make an effort to contact me; I assured them I would check in every couple of months. The Ilikai unit, as well as all subsequent properties, was purchased in my real name, so it was unlikely management could have found me even if they tried. I had several reasons for using my birth name: if for some reason Candi became suspicious and started checking public records she wouldn't find any real estate titled to a familiar name. Also, if I was busted the Feds wouldn't find any property matching the name on the driver's license or social security card I carried, so they wouldn't be able to confiscate my real estate holdings. In the event I turned up dead, my parents would become the beneficiaries of my estate, since the management company had instructions to get in touch with me at my father's west Texas address. My father and I have the same names; I left off the junior part of my name when I contacted the management company and began buying real estate. I left a set of instructions with the management company in a sealed envelope stipulating the envelope was to be opened in case of death or after one year without any contact from me.

With money in the bank, Candi wasted little time and started to plan on how to spend it. Born to successful parents, Candi had enjoyed the advantages and opportunities their economic and social status provided. Traveling abroad was something most young girls never experience, but her parents traveled extensively. She once told me she visited over thirty countries by age ten. Now she was longing to revisit some of the places she remembered visiting as a young girl—the way she described some of the places made them sound like scenes straight out of a fairy tale. In order to revisit the places she remembered from her childhood we needed passports.

After looking over the passport applications we had second thoughts, but decided to go for them anyway. Candi had nothing to lose by using her own birth certificate; I, however, by using the birth certificate of my dead biker buddy from Wyoming, would be taking an unnecessary risk, but I figured what the hell. There seemed to be only two solutions—we could either apply separately or get married (passport applications required proof of marriage if you were applying as husband and wife). We figured it would be simpler just to get married. I knew the marriage license was just a piece of paper and wouldn't change anything between us one way or another.

I figured an address in the same building on the beach in Waikiki where Hollywood types owned property might look impressive on our passport applications, so we moved into a furnished two-bedroom condominium at the Ilikai; Candi thought we were renting—she had no idea I owned it. Over a month passed and we had yet to receive our passports. I was beginning to think the Feds were scrutinizing our credentials a little too closely. I was getting a bit jittery and began taking a different route each time I left the apartment. I wouldn't go as far as to say paranoia was setting in, but all the symptoms were there. I suspected any tourist I saw for a second time of being FBI, but I was suspicious for nothing. Six weeks, almost to the day, after we sent in our applications, our passports arrived in the mail.

By this time our entire crop had sold and we were rolling in money—Candi didn't know the half of it. I had added another twenty thousand to each of the two bank accounts I had in Kaneohe and I now owned two other properties besides the one in the Ilikai; one in the Four Paddle on Kuhio Avenue, and one in the Waikiki Shores. Waikiki Shores, one of the first condominiums built in Waikiki, was an unattractive three-story concrete building, but it had the advantage of being right on the beach—five years later I would own six single-family residential properties in Waikiki, three in Kailua, and an apartment building in Honolulu.

With passports now in hand, Candi started planning our European trip. I insisted on two things: first we purchase round-trip tickets and second, we leave five thousand dollars in our joint bank account. When we returned flat broke, and I knew we would, I didn't want to end up living in a tent on the beach again; neither did I want to give Candi any clues that would lead her to believe I was holding out on her by mysteriously coming up with enough money to rent an apartment.

A month later, just after midnight, we left Honolulu International on an Eastern Airlines flight bound for Frankfurt, Germany. After layovers in Los Angeles and New York we arrived just after 10 a.m. local time. At the Fruehaufen we traded dollars for Deutschmarks at one of the numerous money exchange windows, then one floor below street level we boarded a train to Nuremberg, Bavaria.

When we purchased our three-month rail pass Candi had insisted we go first class; she might have been only a little girl when she traveled Europe with her parents, but she knew what she was doing when it came to rail travel. She also knew what she was doing when it came to accommodations—we rarely stayed in hotels, and more often than not we rented rooms in family homes, which I learned is a very common practice.

From Nuremberg we took the train to Garmish Partenkirchen, where Candi found a *Zimmer* free for two nights. After a short walk from our Zimmer the next morning we had coffee and strudel at a *Konditorei* before we climbed onto a tour bus near the Bahnhof. Our first stop on the tour was Neuschwanstein. From the moment the castle came into view I kept thinking I'd seen it before, which of course was impossible. After we toured the castle and were walking down the hill to where our tour bus was parked, I told Candi I'd seen Neuschwanstein before, but I had never been to Germany. I asked her if she believed in reincarnation and if she thought it possible I had lived here in a past life. She giggled and asked, "Have you ever been to Disneyland?"

For three and a half months I came to know the Candi that might have been and I have no doubt she could have achieved any goal she set for herself had she not been so naive her freshman summer—I wondered how many others, just like Candi, had been robbed of a happy and productive life by the '60s' counterculture. She was brilliant; obviously she'd retained everything she'd learned in school and while traveling with her parents. She knew more about European history than I knew about my hometown. She was a mathematical whiz; she could convert one country's currency to another in her head before the moneychangers could do it on their machines. When we purchased a meal, a room for the night, or tickets for a tour she could give you the dollar value down to the penny, no matter the currency or exchange rate. She spoke enough Italian, French, and German to get us whatever we needed—I was in awe of her.

As we meandered through the gardens of Schönbrunn in Vienna Candi became the historian and schooled me on the Habsburg Empire. And so it went—she gave me a running account of local history no matter where we were; it was like having my own personal tour guide. As we sat on the Spanish Steps in Rome eating *gelato*, she explained that although the steps were built by Italians, and named for the nearby Spanish embassy, the cost of construction was paid for by the French. While we stood on one of the battle towers of the medieval city of Carcassonne, Candi explained why people lived in walled cities, tilling the fields by day and returning to the fortress at night for safety. For a moment a serious expression I had never seen before contorted her face and she said, "Somewhere in the future survival may depend upon the concept of walled cities." Her mood and the moment passed before I could ask the obvious question and I let her statement pass without any comments of my own. As we strolled through the Alcazar in Seville and the Alhambra in Granada she explained in detail how Moslem Arabs, in a mere twenty-five years, had swarmed out of Syria conquering everything from Russia to North Africa, and then crossed the straits of Gibraltar into Spain pushing all the way to the Pyrenees. While in Paris Candi kept taking about the French revolution and on the Place de la Concorde she pointed to a spot where some little French girl was guillotined because she didn't know the difference between bread and cake—I think it had to do with class envy and the fact that the French were always bickering between themselves. I wasn't all that interested in the things she had to say about the French; I didn't care for their surliness.

I think she was truly happy, or at least as happy as she would ever be, during our visit to Europe—Candi referred to it as "the Continent". As the scenes changed I experienced her many moods. She was a little girl again as we fed pigeons in front of San Marco in Venice. As singing gondoliers poled us along the canals she was the romantic Candi. At dinner in Caffé Florian's, a haunt of Valentino, she was the flirtatious Candi.

We arrived back in Frankfort six hours before we were to board the Eastern Airline DC-10 that would take us to JFK International and eventually back to Honolulu. When we stepped off the train at the Fruehaufen Candi insisted we have one last dinner in Europe. We took the escalator to ground level and passed all the currency left over from the countries we had visited through a window to an unsmiling money changer—I don't recall having seen a smiling money changer. They were pleasant but went about their business seriously. We ended up with nearly three hundred Deutschmarks, enough for a nice dinner with a few marks left over. We took another escalator to the next level, where Candi surprised me by choosing a Chinese restaurant—I surmised she would select German or French or at least something European. When I asked why Chinese, she moved close and said, "It looks romantic and I thought an intimate setting would be nice for our last evening in Europe." Anytime Candi became warm and affectionate I started thinking ahead—ecstasy awaited, the only question was when and where. She looked at me with those big sparkling eyes and moved even closer, her soft body pressing against mine and when I asked if she was a member of the mile-high club, a devilish little grin stole across her lips and she answered, "Not yet."

With candles, white tablecloths, and napkins on ebony tables secluded in nooks and alcoves, tuxedoed waiters, and barely audible music, it was indeed romantic. What started out as dinner became an enchanting evening; it was as though a spell had been cast over us. As flickering candlelight cast shadows across our faces and our minds, soft strains of alien refrains played on unfamiliar instruments muted all sound beyond our personal space. We reverted to our days of innocence, relived our childhoods as we laughed about monsters that lived under our beds and how we escaped disconcerting sounds in the night by hiding under the covers. We talked about friends, birthday parties, and Christmas dinners. We shared our dreams, our goals; we speculated on what we thought life would be like as we evolved and how we would look when we grew old. Even the waiter was unable to break the spell by presenting the check; the mood carried over and even as we exited the restaurant, it was as though we had known each other all our lives and had skipped from childhood to this very moment with only good times in between.

We were still caught up in our fantasy as we exited the restaurant and made the trip back down to the money changer. We gave him all the marks we had left and exchanged them for greenbacks. We ended up with more than I expected; we had enough for snacks during layovers at JFK and Los Angeles and a taxi when we got back to Honolulu. While we stood waiting to board, Candi pressed against me with just enough movement to convey her emotional state.

Shortly after the Fasten Seatbelts sign was turned off Candi released her seatbelt, leaned close, flashed her devilish little grin, crooked her finger a couple of times in a follow-me gesture, and exited her seat. The restroom was small and cramped, but as the big jet climbed out over France we became mile-high club members, and somewhere over the Atlantic we became five-mile-high club members.

Busted

By now, anytime we returned from off Island, our first night back in paradise had become a ritual—a frolic on the beach, which continued at the Lewers Street hotel, followed by an evening at Trader Vic's, and an after-dinner romp in our room. The next morning I pulled the last one-hundred-dollar bill hidden in the toe of my boot and gave it to Candi—I had used the one I had stuck in the toe of my other boot to pay for the evening at Trader Vic's. She grinned and said, "I knew you were holding out on me," and gave me a big kiss while I copped a feel; she then hurried off toward the beach. I headed for a meeting with my partners.

The meeting went well; my partners were as eager to get started as always and handed over my cash advance first thing. When I told them I had some new ideas and might need some additional up-front money, they doubled the previous year's seed money without even asking what I had in mind. Needless to say, my partners knew they had a sweet deal and wanted to hold on to it; I was doing fairly well myself.

My new idea was to use the Waihole Ditch to move our paco lolo bricks from the windward side of the island, where the jungle provided ideal conditions for growing and hid growers from prying eyes, to the leeward side, where narcs weren't likely to be watching. The Feds had stepped up their efforts on Oahu and were using helicopters to spot growers backpacking their crops down the mountain and they also waited in strategic locations along the Kamehameha Highway hoping to catch farmers loading marijuana into vehicles.

It seemed like the perfect system—I had to reflect only on Operation Quick Rich to realize when you start thinking a scheme is perfect you are in for a lot of disappointment. Nevertheless, it seemed a lot safer than playing hide and seek with the choppers and unmarked patrol cars along the Kam.

When sugar cane was king, someone came up with the idea of digging a tunnel through the mountains and siphoning off water from the windward side, where it rained every day, to the leeward side, where growing conditions for sugar cane were good except for the lack of water—the weather forecast on Oahu is the same every day, "Sunny with windward and *mauka* (mountain) showers." Rainfall on the windward side is 60 to 100 inches a year, more than enough to sustain a lush green jungle, while the leeward side of the island averaged 9 inches of precipitation a year and was a brown desertlike plane with cactus and a few scrub trees.

After stumbling onto the Waihole Ditch I did a little research and found that the Oahu Sugar Company (OSCo) had started building the Ditch in 1913 and finished sometime in 1916. The Ditch was built to irrigate a sugar cane plantation owned and operated by OSCo.

I talked with a few locals about the tunnel and learned that teenagers sometimes floated the tunnel when the water was low. Several of those I talked with knew of someone who had floated through the mountain, but none claimed to have done it themselves. It seemed so simple it just might work; all I had to do was seal the bricks in plastic, dump them into the Ditch and let the water do the rest. It would be just a matter of time before the bricks would pop out on the leeward side of the island.

This was only half of my plan. Backpacking the bricks down the mountain was a lot of work and it was during this time I was most vulnerable. If you were unlucky enough to be spotted by someone inside a helicopter you had to stash your backpack and hope you could evade the Feds on the ground—if you did manage to escape it wasn't likely your paco lolo would be where you left it when you returned.

As luck would have it, the lava tubes I used for growing were only a few hundred yards east and about 1000 feet up the side of the mountain above the entrance to the main bore, but getting the bricks to the Ditch was the hardest part. Backpacking them down that particular area of the Koolau was next to impossible. However, I had no intentions of climbing up and down the mountain carrying marijuana. I intended to stretch a wire strong enough to handle the load, but thin enough not to catch the eyes of federal agents inside a helicopter.

It was a lot of work. By harvest time I had the wires in place, but toward the end I was beginning to wonder if it would be worth all the effort I put into it. Clearing a tunnel through undergrowth to make sure the bricks had a clear path to slide down the wires was the worst part; I vowed never to touch another machete for the rest of my life. Due to the topography and dense undergrowth it was impossible to run a single wire all the way down the mountain. It took seven sections to get to a spot just above the tunnel in the midst of dense jungle that would keep my operation hidden. Another problem was to keep the bricks from gathering too much speed before they hit the bottom of any given run. Without a braking system my crop would end up spread all over the mountainside. I designed and tested several sophisticated systems which all failed; in the end I used Penn International deep-sea fishing reels with 100-pound Dacron line. The Penn reels had sufficient braking power without fading or burning out the brake—simple works every time. This allowed me to ease fifty bricks at a time down the wire—I still referred to them as bricks, but in order to get our paco lolo safely through the tunnel without getting it wet required encasing it in plastic; 2-gallon Zip-Lock baggies worked perfectly. When the bricks reached the bottom of one section of wire I climbed down and attached them to the reel on the next section and repeated this until I reached the area of thick jungle just above the tunnel. From there it was a simple matter of carrying the bricks a few yards before dropping them over the gate at the tunnel's entrance and letting the water do the rest—the steel bars in the gate were wide enough apart to allow the baggies to float through, but I wasn't taking any chances. Then I climbed back up and started another load down the mountain. When the bricks popped out of the tunnel on the other side of the mountain my partners were waiting with dip nets.

On the way back up I stopped at the head of each wire run and reeled the line in, which brought the carrier system back to the top and ready for the next time I started a load down the wires. I sent the bricks down the wires on rainy or foggy days, when I could see to navigate the treacherous climb, but visibility for DEA using choppers or telescopes was limited. I sent two loads down a day; when the second load was safely in the tunnel I hiked out to the Kam and walked or hitchhiked to Punaluu, where Candi and I rented a place on the beach. When my partners arranged for another sale I climbed back up the Koolua and sent two more loads down the wires and into the tunnel.

Candi would crank up the Rusty Bucket in the predawn hours, drive down the Kam, and drop me off in an isolated spot, from where I hiked back to the tunnel and started the climb up the mountain, reeling up the carriers as I climbed. Upon reaching the lava tubes I lit off a propane burner and set a bucket of wax over the flame. Then I stuffed a hundred baggies with marijuana leaves from the drying tables—the hydro-driven alternator system that supplied heat for my plant beds also supplied heat for drying tables. By the time I finished stuffing the baggies the wax had melted; I then opened the zip lock on one of the baggies an inch or so, dropped in a couple of small packages containing silica granules, squeezed out as much of the air as I could, zipped it shut and dipped the zip-lock edge of the bag into the hot wax, let the wax cool and harden, then dipped it a second time, and let it cool again before setting it aside and repeating the process ninety-nine more times.

With the baggies filled, sealed, and ready to go I emptied the leaves from one of the air-drying bins onto the heated tables. When the first plants were ready for harvesting I would start stripping and putting the leaves into wire cages which I rotated regularly to keep air passing through the leaves. With this process I was able to bring paco lolo to market with considerable lower moisture content than my competitors; this alone commanded a higher price.

I finished spreading the leaves on the drying tables and rotated the bins several times before taking my lunch break. It was well past noon before I started my first fifty bricks down the wire; it would be another six hours before I dumped the second load into the Ditch.

This system worked well for four years, but toward the end of our fifth season someone found a baggie downstream of the tunnel and turned it over to HPD. It didn't take long for the authorities to figure out what was going on. Before we reached the spot where Candi normally dropped me off, we saw a helicopter with a searchlight working the area above the tunnel. We just kept on driving until we reached Kaneohe, where we stopped for breakfast at Perry's. After we paid and found a table Candi picked up a plate and headed for the fruit bar, while I used a nearby pay phone to call my partners; needless to say, they were disappointed at hearing the news. We agreed to meet later in the day and figure out what to do—there was no need to mention the location of the meeting place.

I sat on the uppermost section of the Natatorium looking out at the Pacific Ocean thinking about nothing in particular when I saw my partners approaching. They climbed up and sat down beside me. Neither one said anything; they just sat there with their heads down, looking glum. Finally I broke the silence. "I guess this means we're going to have to lie low for a while."

They nodded in unison. "Well, we lost only half our crop; it could have been worse."

The brothers nodded again, but still didn't look up or speak. I waited for a minute or more before saying, "We need to talk about money."

Finally the older brother broke their silence, "We got your share, we won't do you wrong."

"I know you won't."

The younger brother handed me a brown canvas bag and said, "We decided to split it sixty-forty, sixty for you, forty for us."

"That's not the deal; I'm only in for half."

"We know, man, but you do all the work, and besides we think we're responsible for the bust."

"How so?"

"When we rendezvoused with a buyer about three weeks ago and counted out, we were one baggie short. We figure one of the baggies got hung up in the tunnel and came out after we left, or we missed one as they came through. We suspect someone found it downstream and handed it over to the Feds; either way, we figured it's our fault."

"Why didn't you warn me?"

"We were afraid you would quit us; we were hoping nothing would come of it. You mad at us, man?"

"Nah, I'm not mad, hell, it's about time I took some time off anyway. We'll just lie low for a couple of years and start up in another location. Does that work for you?"

"It works for us, man. Just let us know when you're ready." We talked a bit longer, then shook hands and went our separate ways. A week passed before it made the news. There were pictures of the wire system and speculation on how the Waihole Ditch had been used to float paco lolo from one side of the island to the other. The estimated street value of the abandoned marijuana, according to the Feds, was in excess of a half million dollars.

I let Candi think I was successful in getting only about 25 percent of our crop off the mountain. I gave her seventy thousand with instructions to put only a few thousand at a time in our joint bank account. I spent the next two weeks putting money in my bank accounts. Every day I'd put somewhere between seven and nine thousand dollars in each of my accounts—the banks routinely report deposits of ten grand or more to the IRS.

Candi was already figuring out how to spend *her* share of the profits. Anytime we had money or anything of value it was hers—it was never ours. She still didn't know, or even suspect I was holding out on her. I suggested we should buy one of the units in the condominium where we were staying—I already had several properties, but I thought it would be good for Candi if she had a place of her own and a sense of putting down roots. I was surprised when she agreed.

Pat's at Punaluu was a five-year-old, rather plain concrete structure built right on the beach. There had been a flurry of sales the first year, but interest cooled and unit prices were only slightly higher than when they first hit the market. We had been renting an efficiency unit on the lower level, but I convinced Candi we should lay out forty-six thousand dollars for an upper-level one-bedroom unit on the ocean side. When Candi wrote a check for the entire amount, the real estate agent gave her a questioning second look; she probably knew the source of the money but wasn't about to blow a sale by inquiring about something that wasn't any of her business. Candi spent another ten grand furnishing *her* new condo and after we moved in she seemed quite pleased with the idea of owning *her* own place.

By paying cash for the unit our only expenses, aside from utilities, were monthly dues paid to the homeowners association for maintenance and upkeep plus a small leasehold fee. Candi already had more than twenty thousand dollars in her account before I gave her the extra seventy thousand, so I figured we could live comfortably for a couple of years before setting up another growing operation. I wasn't all that anxious to get back into the poco lolo business, and in hindsight, I should have called it quits and told Candi about my bank accounts and the real estate I owned. Within a few years we could have parlayed my holdings into a financial position where we wouldn't have needed to worry about being destitute in our old age. But I couldn't bring myself to fully trust Candi; she had never given me reason not to trust her, but there was something about her I couldn't put my finger on that troubled me. Perhaps it was her philosophy.

Candi's socialist tendencies were always at war with her own greed and she had mixed emotions anytime we checked into a luxury hotel, ate at a gourmet restaurant, or traveled first class. She loved the accommodations, but hated everyone, especially her parents, who could legitimately afford to live the life she couldn't. She theorized that everyone should share equally and freely in everything. I had at one time believed Candi incapable of happiness no matter the circumstances, and thought she just wanted others to share in her misery. But there were times when I thought she was happy, at least as happy as she could be. And after the purchase of the condo came one of those times. Her attitude changed. I wouldn't go so far as to say Candi had turned 180 degrees in her view of the way things ought to be, but it was quite evident by the way she elegantly decorated her new home that she took pride in ownership—she could probably have made a good living as an interior decorator.

Candi had grown up in a cultured environment and it showed in everything she did. There was a refinement about her and little by little it rubbed off on me—by association I had grown. I knew I couldn't protect her from herself, but I would take care of her as best I could as long as she would let me. I loved her, but I didn't trust her.

Candi taught me many things, but in turn I was unable to instill any degree of self-worth in her or persuade her to pursue life with a positive attitude and purpose rather than wallow in negativity and self-pity. There were short periods of time when I was successful, but in the end I would be the recipient of her wrath for questioning her opinions and way of life.

It wasn't long, however, before the demons that haunted Candi and ruled her life took over again. A couple of months later, out of the clear blue she said, "I'm tired of this place, let's go to one of the other Islands."

"What's wrong with it? I thought you liked it."

"Did you know my bedroom was larger than this entire unit? My bathroom was bigger than our bedroom."

"What was and what is are two different things. This place is a giant step up from the house trailer you were renting in Tacoma."

"I don't care; I want to go to a different Island." She continued with a comment she knew would hurt me.

"If you hadn't blown Operation Quick Rich we could live anywhere we want." I wanted to tell her the truth, and if things had continued the way they had for the last few months, and in the right setting, I might have revealed the extent of my holdings to her— they were now worth way more than she had thought we were going to embezzle from Northwest Orient, but her statement reaffirmed what I already knew—she could never know.

A couple of days later, after listing her unit as a *completely furnished, read-to-move-into condo*, we paid the Young Brothers Barge Company to transport the Rusty Bucket, and then boarded a plane to Kauai—before boarding I called my broker and instructed him to buy Candi's unit, but not rent it out; I wanted it to be exactly the way she left it just in case she changed her mind later on.

We found parts of Kauai less than friendly, and there were too many hardcore weirdos on the Pali Coast, so after a few months we put the Rusty Bucket on the barge again and headed for the Big Island. I was happy when Candi suggested we leave Kauai. I was hoping after a few months on the Big Island she would become disenchanted with roaming from Island to Island and suggest we move back to Oahu—another dream that would never become reality.

Information circulating in any society depends upon the interests of a particular group and varies from one to another, so it is of little wonder that we were drawn to the hippie community of Pahoa Town—an area near where Highway 130 eventually heads up into the Hawaii Volcanoes National Park through the ocean community of Kalapona.

Various communities on the Big Island flourished while sugarcane was king, but families relocated after growing operations moved off Island, leaving many company towns in a state of disrepair. Hippies, taking advantage of cheap housing, began moving into the rundown houses and stores in Pahoa Town. While some simply squatted, others purchased property and began making repairs. In a relatively short time the town was sporting a new look with boardwalks, flowers, and fresh paint complete with murals in psychedelic hues. New entrepreneurs opened their doors with a different look and a different way of doing business. Incense permeated the small-scale co-ops with handmade gifts and paintings by resident artists as well as the mini boutiques featuring peasant skirts and blouses with matching jewelry, all handmade within the community—tie-dyed tank tops and tee shirts were big sellers. A grocery store and a couple of small restaurants opened for business. It goes without saying, paco lolo could be purchased anywhere in town—school children were well aware Pahoa Town kids had *crazy weed* for sale.

Word of the town's renaissance spread and before long, Islanders from as far away as Hilo and Kailua Kona were frequenting Pahoa Town; whether by accident or design, Hippie Town soon became a tourist stop.

By the time we arrived on the scene, most of the choice property had been bought up by early-arriving hippies; the few parcels still available were now in the hands of real estate speculators. Candi, still flush from the sale of her condo, called the number of the real estate agent posted in the window of a small two-bedroom house on the edge of town, and early next morning we met in his Hilo office, where she wrote a check for the asking price with only one stipulation—she would be allowed to move in immediately. Two phone calls later, one to the bank and one to the seller, and it was a done deal—an hour later we were on a plane to Honolulu.

It was early in the afternoon when we arrived at the Ala Moana shopping center, where Candi dropped five grand in less than three hours. We took a break while enjoying an early dinner at Keo's before Candi resumed her spending spree. By the time we climbed into a taxi that would take us back to the airport she had laid out another twenty-five hundred dollars. We caught the last flight back to Hilo and called it a day.

Structurally, the little house was in remarkably good condition—providing you overlooked termite damage—and required only minor repairs. We replaced a few outside boards, made a number of interior changes, gave it a good paint job inside and out, and by the end of the week had it looking pretty good. We finished none too soon; Candi had paid to have her purchases packed and shipped to her new digs in Pahoa Town and on Monday afternoon, a day after we finished painting, a truck arrived with all her stuff.

By the end of the following week Candi had her flower-child pad just the way she wanted it. I awoke the next morning (Saturday) just in time to watch Candi add the finishing touches to her gypsy outfit.

"How do I look?" she asked, performing a tour *en l'air*; her skirt fanned out, revealing that she wore no panties—the most casual observer would know she was braless.

"Very sexy," I exclaimed as I tried to grab her and pull her onto the bed. But she was too quick for me and floated away with a *jete*, and then performing an *entrechant* she clicked her heels together three times, as though laughing at me, before lightly touching down. Candi was enjoying herself. I figured in her mind she was reliving her teenage years, mixing junior high with her early days as a new bohemian—I surmised the entire Pahoa Town experiment was an attempt to escape back to those earlier days she remembered as her *good old days*. She finished off her performance with a wink, a smile, and a *plie* before disappearing into the second bedroom through beaded curtains that served as a door—all interior doors had been replaced with multiple strands of colored beads.

I pulled on a pair of cutoffs and passed through another beaded curtain into a single room about 12 feet deep that spanned the entire width of the house and served as living room, dining room, and kitchen. Two doors opening into the bedrooms were set side by side in the wall opposite the front door. I poured myself a cup of coffee, dumped some cereal in a bowl with some milk, and sat down to breakfast. I hadn't paid any attention to Candi's new decorations while I was putting breakfast together, but now I sat looking around the room in amazement. It was a scene out of "Carmen" or perhaps "Aleko." As I sat awestruck by Candi's handiwork she emerged from the second bedroom, saw me and asked, "What do you think?"

She held up a 12-by-36 inch board attractively painted with a mysterious-looking design and the words, "Tarot Readings" printed in an exotic script.

I laughed, "You can't read tarot cards."

"Can too," she countered defiantly as she leaned forward and with a sexy back-and-forth wiggle stuck out her tongue.

I tried to grab her, but she danced away and stuck out her tongue again.

She hung the sign in the window and then stuck out her tongue for a third time before disappearing back into the second bedroom.

I finished breakfast, cleaned off the table, washed and put the dishes away, then walked over, parted the beaded curtain and stuck my head inside the second bedroom. My jaw dropped and I guess my mouth fell open as well; the sweet fragrance of sandalwood drifted out of brass incense burners, the strains of soft soulful guitars and violins emanated from hidden speakers, candles flickered in brass candelabras. I could have been in Zoltar's reading room.

Surprisingly, to me anyway, tourists were in fact willing to pay Candi for a reading; she actually made enough money to keep her in incense and candles with a little left over for groceries. Nevertheless, Candi's bank account had dropped below ten thousand dollars for the first time since we left Oahu—as far as she knew that was the only money we had—and at the rate it was going one more trip off Island and we would be penniless. Once again I was faced with the dilemma of telling Candi about my real estate holdings or going back into pot farming. It had been two years since the close call in Kahana Valley and I figured it would be safe to start up my growing operation again since no one but my former partners could connect me to the marijuana trade—there were those who suspected, but none were sure.

When I informed Candi I was going back into business and intended to spend half the money we had on a used boat and trailer she merely responded with body language which I knew meant it was okay—I conveniently left out the fact I'd already bought a 15-foot Zodiac Grand Raid with twin 25-horse Mercury outboards and an easy-lift trailer.

Candi was no fool, she knew what provided her with the money she enjoyed spending. She also knew if we eliminated partners we could keep all the profit for ourselves; greed ruled many of Candi's decisions so she quickly agreed to go it alone; she would contact buyers and set up times and places for the transfer of goods and money. The more we talked the more excited she became; she liked the idea of personally handling tens of thousands, perhaps even hundreds of thousands of dollars. I told her we had enough money to start up the following spring, which wasn't true for what I had in mind, but unlike the first year when we arrived in The Islands almost broke, I had plenty of capital. But I would let Candi believe we were working with the money in her bank account.

Marijuana had replaced sugarcane as the money crop on the Big Island; all the well-hidden growing areas with easy access had already been claimed and were fearlessly defended to the point of shooting wars. Several people had disappeared simply because they inadvertently wandered into someone's *patch*. Most of the established growers had formed a co-op. Although they didn't share their profits with one another, they were tight knit and worked as a group to promote their product. These growers all lived in million-dollar homes built on past marijuana sales; prior to harvest one of the growers—they took turns—would open his home and host a party for major buyers complete with champagne, hors d'oeuvres, girls to entertain, and of course, paco lolo. The growers all brought and displayed samples, bids were accepted, contracts were let and sealed with handshakes and up-front money—these buyers were mostly from California with several Hollywood types thrown into the mix. Word was, local law enforcement agencies were paid to turn a blind eye to these parties and it was generally understood, if one wanted to stay out of trouble with the law, it wasn't wise to compete with this group of growers. I didn't want any part of that scene; I intended to find some rugged area off the beaten path where I could run my type of operation without local intervention.

About two weeks after I'd decided to go back into the paco lolo trade I loaded five 6-gallon gas tanks onto the Grand Raid and strapped them down behind the rear seat to prevent the tanks from drifting around inside the boat in case we got into rough seas. Although a neat setup, I found it strange that a rubber boat with air chambers should have a polished mahogany floor and seats. I covered the half dozen waterproof bags I'd placed forward of the bow seat with a tarp, and tied them down. Four bags contained our camping gear and enough food for a couple of weeks; the other two bags were filled with clothes and who knows what. I secured Candi's surfboard to the seat amidships and announced, "I'm finished; you about ready?"

"Give me another minute."

The rear springs on the Rusty Bucket were just about bottomed out, but since I planned to launch at Hilo I figured we'd be okay for that distance. I slipped in under the wheel when I saw Candi come out of the house and lock the door; she climbed into the passenger seat and asked, "What's the hold-up?"

I looked at her and grinned without answering. She slipped across the seat, gave my inner thigh a little squeeze and asked, "Is that better?" I just kept on grinning as I started the old Chevy and eased along the narrow strip of dirt that served as our driveway until I reached the road and then turned toward Hilo.

I put into a small, almost hidden cove cut into the rugged cliffs between the Waipio and Pololu valleys, eased back on the power and cruised to within 50 feet of a waterfall at the head of the cove before running the bow of the Zodiac onto the beach. I killed the ignition, stepped out onto the sand, walked 20 feet up the beach, threw a line around an Australian pine standing just above the tide line, and tied off with a half hitch.

The little cove was perfect for exchanging large quantities of paco lolo for duffle bags filled with hundred-dollar bills. And with the waterfall coming directly out of the cliff face I had good reason to believe there would be numerous lava tubes, some of which would be ideal for what I had in mind, an operation similar to the one I had set up on windward Oahu. Candi stripped off her clothes, grabbed her board and headed for the surf; I untied the tarp, carried our supplies up the beach to the edge of the trees, and set up camp. After smearing on some bug dope and sunscreen I picked up a pair of 10-by-50 Lica binoculars and walked back down the beach to the Grand Raid, climbed inside, sat down on the floor, stretched out, and leaned back against one of the air chambers. I spent a couple of hours scanning the cliffs, sketching maps, and writing notes on 3-by-5 cards before the warm rays of a lazy afternoon sun, combined with the rhythm of waves breaking every so softly as they moved ocean grinders up and down the beach worked their magic.

I awoke to cold water dripping on my nose and forehead. I opened my eyes to see Candi leaning over me dangling her wet hair in my face. I grabbed her and pulled her into the boat, she landed on top of me and I wrapped my arms around her, holding her wet, naked body close to mine.

"Your skin is freezing, aren't you cold?"

"A little," she flashed that devilish little grin and asked, "Do you think can you warm me up?"

She pulled away, bounced out of the Grand Raid, and ran for the tent; I caught up just as she unzipped the mosquito netting and darted inside.

I figured if I was going to start up another growing operation I might as well get the maximum benefit for my efforts and grow year around; dealers would be eager to buy anything available in the off-season. They would also be willing to pay a higher price—supply and demand played its part in all segments of the economy.

Although marijuana was known to the Chinese five thousand years ago and spread into India shortly thereafter, it had taken another thirty-five hundred years before it reached Europe via the route of Muslim invaders through North Africa. Three hundred fifty years later marijuana was part of America's pharmacopeia and was prescribed for several ailments. I was just a kid when World War II ended, but in the early '40s I remember an uncle smoking tobacco, or so I thought at the time, with a weird aroma—he claimed it was for asthma—it came both loose and ready-rolled, and with a prescription it could be purchased at the drugstore. It wasn't until the end of my first season with Weyerhaeuser when Krocker and I headed down California's Highway 1 and I lit up my first reefer that I realized what my uncle had been smoking—I'd always wondered why he was so laid back.

Be that as it may, it took the Beat Generation of the 1950s to introduce it to the country's youth. By the 1960s it was the recreational drug of choice for flower children and college students and had become one of the symbols of the antiestablishment crowd.

Until the mid-'70s cheap weed poured in from Mexico, but concerns of toxic side effects from the spraying of Mexican crops with the herbicide *paraquat* put a scare into marijuana users in the United States, at which time Colombia became the main supplier for America's youth. Shortly thereafter hybrids came on the scene with names like Panama Red and Acapulco Gold.

At the time I had taken over Krocker's patches and set up my own operation, young people simply wanted weed—potency wasn't an issue. They just wanted to smoke, mellow out, and have sex. Free love was as much a symbol of the dissident lifestyle as were drugs—

tune in, turn on, drop out. But, also, with the coming of the '70s, other, more powerful hallucinogenic drugs with alluring names like Paper Dots (lysergic acid diethylamide, commonly known as LSD), Orange Sunshine, and Chocolate Mescaline, to name a few, began competing with cannabis for a share of the market. As a result, marijuana loyalists were demanding higher levels of tetrahydrocannabional or THC. Along with the sociable smoker were those desiring a mind-altering experience. Almost overnight, or so it seemed, potency became everything and hybrids were developed to answer the call. Many were still happy just smoking *chaff* and kicking back, but mostly, it was about the *bud* (sinsemilla)—bud smokers considered any part of the plant other than bud worthless. Well, if it was bud they wanted, it was bud they'd get, and if it was a mind-altering experience they wanted it was a mind-altering experience they would get. I was more than willing to accommodate.

It had been six months of hard work and cost more than thirty thousand dollars, but everything was falling into place. My operation on Oahu had been first class for the times, but the market had changed almost overnight—I can't say I was ahead of the paradigm shift, but I was keeping up and way out in front of just about every grower in The Islands. I had new *sativa* hybrid seeds, from the Paradise Seed Company of Amsterdam, Holland, sprouting in flats floating in a warm-water nutrient solution—a technique suggested to me by a Tennessee farmer who grew his tobacco sets from seed, then transplanted the plugs after the young seedlings grew to a height of 4 to 6 inches and developed three or four leaves. My hydroponics system was in place; thermostatically controlled water heaters would keep the water at an ideal temperature; pumps would circulate and aerate the heated water underneath peat held up by wire mesh that would serve as support for the plant's root systems. Wires were strung to prevent plants from falling over as they grew and permit better light penetration—numerous reflectors redirected light for maximum efficiency. Hemingway-type overhead fans insured good circulation of air, a precaution against mold and mildew which can devastate a crop in a matter of hours. Buds are susceptible to mold and mildew when lights are turned down to encourage flowering. I eliminated all male plants as soon as they became identifiable and when I set the timers to turn off the lights for prolonged periods to encourage flowering I changed the nutrient solution and added a supplement sold under the name Super Bloom. The fans also served to pull in outside air to keep heat, generated by the lights, from building, but the primary reason was to pull in air heavy with carbon dioxide, a necessary ingredient for photosynthesis. The CO2 was conveniently provided by Mother Nature's compost on the jungle floor outside the lava tube. Heavy blackout curtains would keep the grow lights from attracting the attention of anyone cruising offshore or flying along the cliffs at night. Power lines, concealed beneath dense undergrowth, snaked up the cliff from a hydro-driven generator. The generator, well hidden behind and powered by the waterfall supplied the necessary electricity. There were no telltale signs to hint at the elaborate marijuana-growing operation inside a lava tube 200 feet above the beach.

In the beginning I considered using a heavy-duty motorized wire system similar to the one I'd used on windward Oahu to transport supplies up from the beach and bricks back down to the beach, but I surmised DEA would be watching for anything remotely close to my old system and decided against it. It would mean hundreds of trips up and down the cliff face with a heavy backpack, but why take the chance.

The thought of having a lot of money to spend moved Candi to a level of participation I hadn't seen since Operation Quick Rich. Four months after my first seed popped Candi was on her way to Honolulu with a pocket full of samples for buyers—only known buyers who expressed an interest when previously contacted were provided a sample. Harvesting and drying buds was time consuming and required more work than I anticipated. This required Candi to make dozens of trips to Honolulu; on each trip she carried a daypack filled with bud and deposited a bundle of cash just shy of the amount requiring banks to alert the Feds into her bank account. All money remaining went into her safe-deposit box. Candi was a shrewd businesswoman—after the first couple of deliveries she upped the ante and before she finished selling our crop she had buyers bidding against one another. By the time she made her last sale we had taken in almost six times what I'd made in any given year working with my partners on Oahu.

I dried and pressed the chaff into bricks, packed them down to the beach in waterproof bags, and a guy picked up the entire lot late one night in a big Zodiac. He paid me with a ditty bag full of hundred-dollar bills while a couple of guys loaded the bags of marijuana leaves into the Zodiac; the transfer took less than thirty minutes.

Candi was elated with our success and needless to say, eager to spend the profits. I tried to convince her we should start a winter crop.

"If we grow two crops a year and invest everything we can retire in five years, get completely out of the marijuana business and never worry about security in our old age; by then we'll have more than ten times the amount Northwest Orient gave us"—Candi still believed I got away with two million dollars. Although I didn't want her to know about my investments, I was hopeful that being in charge of sales and bank accounts would instill in her a sense of responsibility and in turn an eye toward her future well-being. I was dreaming the impossible dream; for Candi today, tomorrow at the latest, was the future.

"Old age!" She mouthed the term as though it were a curse you wished on people you loathed. "I'll never see forty." For a moment she appeared to turn against everything she claimed to believe in and reverted to the lifestyle of her heritage.

"I want to get off this boring island. I'm tired of living in a shanty with rats, centipedes, cane spiders, termites, and geckos; I want to live in a real house and feel plush carpet underneath my feet. I want to take baths in Jacuzzi tubs in marble bathrooms with indirect lighting, and I want someone to keep everything clean and orderly. I'm tired of eating fried rice and spam for breakfast, lunch, and dinner; I want gourmet meals prepared by a chef and served on fine china set on white linen tablecloths. I'm tired of sleeping in a leaky waterbed and in a tent on the beach with sand fleas and mosquitoes; I want a king-sized bed with perfumed sheets and down pillows. I want to go to the ballet and the theater on opening night; I'm ready for some culture in my life while I still have time to enjoy it."

I knew I should take the first flight off Island, disappear, and leave Candi to her own devices, but I couldn't. Whether I was indeed under her spell or cursed with the weakness inherent in the masculine gene—the need to take care of helpless women—I'll never know, but I just couldn't leave her.

Two and a half years later we were back on Island broke and not speaking to each another. The cold shoulder didn't last long; it never did. Our place in Pahoa Town was a mess. I had to physically throw out a couple of potheads. It took a week to get it livable. By this time Candi was her old self again, amenable and affectionate and willing to do whatever was necessary to amass enough money to buy another fantasy—in the last two years we had lived a life of leisure steeped in luxury in places I'd only heard about. Most were as unfamiliar to me as the dark side of the moon. I think Candi had decided she could live her fantasy life in installments and when the last episode expired she would accept whatever was to be her fate. I had to admit it was a fantastic two and a half years and for one brief moment I considered selling all my holdings and joining Candi in living the life she wanted until it ran out and then let the taxpayers take care of me in my old age. The daydream gave way to reality and I started preparing for another growing season—once again I found myself hoping I could talk some sense into Candi and this would be the last crop; I was tired of looking over my shoulder all the time.

Candi was eager to resume her role as business manager and pretty soon had spread the word we would have a crop ready for market in about four months. She already had several orders lined up when the guy who bought the chaff from my last crop offered to take everything if we could have it all ready for a one-time pickup. He was also willing to pay up-front money for the right to buy the entire crop. I had planned to operate the same as before with Candi delivering the bud a backpack full at a time, but something had changed and it worried me. The Department of Agriculture had started using beagles to sniff out illegal produce in tourist's luggage on the way back to the mainland and I was afraid they might extend the little hounds' duties to checking bags coming into Honolulu from outer Islands. Although I'd dealt with him before, I never liked the guy, but he always showed up on time and paid top dollar, so I took the deal. Candi collected the down payment and stashed it in her safe-deposit box. Although I now vacuum-packed the bricks, making them more difficult to detect by smell alone, taking the deal seemed a lot safer than running the risk of getting busted by a beagle. The guy was not only connected but the relative of a powerful politician, which was another reason I took the deal. He never worried about getting busted.

The current crop was better than my last; I hadn't had any problem with mold or mildew or pests that can devastate a crop. The drying had gone well and I was delivering a superior product. The guy was excited when he checked the samples and was eager to complete the deal. Candi gave him a date and he picked the time, she told him it would be in the exact same spot where he'd picked up the chaff from my last crop.

The sun was hanging only a few degrees above the jagged peaks of the Kohala Mountains by the time I reached the narrow strip of sand separating the jungle from the Pacific Ocean—evening was on its way, with night not far behind. I stopped in a dense area of palms and deposited my last load of bricks inside a wooden crate with the rest of the bags, and then replaced the palm fronds to camouflage the box before heading for the beach.

It had been a long day and I was ready for some rest and relaxation. The relaxation I had in mind had just caught a wave about 30 yards out—waves broke close to shore in this little cove. Candi was a sun worshiper with long black hair and was often mistaken for a local. Her evenly tanned body, glowing golden in the lingering rays of sunlight as she slipped her board along the face of the wave, was a testament to her love of nature and disdain for swimsuits. As I watched her work the wave, I wondered what I would have been doing, where I would have been, and what my life would have been like had that fateful meeting which seemed like only yesterday, but in reality was a lifetime ago never occurred. She spotted me and headed toward the beach. When the wave petered out she eased herself into the water and waded ashore, walked up the beach to within 3 feet of where I sat, dropped her board onto the sand and slowly sank to her knees. Her eyes sparkled as she asked, "You tired?"

"Not that tired." I answered.

That devilish little smile I had come to know so well played across her lips as she arched her body and leaned backward. Tilting her head even further back she brought both arms up and while reaching behind her head gathered up her hair and gave it a couple of twists before bringing it around in front of her. She gave it a few more twists to squeeze out the water, and then leaning forward, let go of her hair, shook it loose and as she straightened up, tossed her head, flipping the hair behind her back.

"Race you to the shower." She sprang to her feet and was off and running before I could move. She dove into the pool below the waterfall just as I caught up to her. I swam underneath the curtain of tumbling water to an area where I kept soap and other personal hygiene items. I lathered up and scrubbed the sweat and grime off my body using spray from the waterfall as a shower, shampooed my hair, and scraped off my beard with a razor in bad need of a new blade. I brushed my teeth and then eased into the water and swam back underneath the waterfall just as Candi walked out onto the beach. She saw me and ran for the tent. I took my time. There was no need to hurry—she would be there waiting for me.

One Last Taste of Candi

It was sometime after midnight when I heard the soft gurgling sounds of the powerful outboard motors. I tried to disentangle myself from Candi without waking her, but she bolted upright at my first movement. Upon hearing the outboard motors she stiffened momentarily, then threw herself at me and wrapped her arms around me for several seconds before pulling away; she then dropped back onto the blanket and pulled it over her naked body.

After applying a generous amount of bug repellent I slipped on my cutoffs and a tanktop before unzipping the mosquito netting and stepping out onto the sand. Using a piece of driftwood I punched up the fire then, tossed the driftwood onto the remaining embers and added two more pieces to insure we would have enough light to do business; a few seconds later the fire came to life and within a minute flames were leaping a couple of feet into the air.

The outboard motors where silent now. I turned my back to the fire and stared out through the darkness toward the beach where I surmised the crew was pulling a large Zodiac onto the sand. My thoughts returned to Candi and how weird she'd been since her last trip to Honolulu; actually, she had been acting strange for the last couple of months, but her actions at the airport when she returned three weeks ago bordered on bizarre.

Normally, when she returned from a trip she hurried over, snuggled up, and engaged me in a series of passionate kisses between whispers of promised ecstasy. We would then get her bags, throw them into the back seat of the Rusty Bucket and head for home in Pahoa Town.

But this time when she got off the plane she'd just stood there at the bottom of the stairs looking at me. I thought I had seen and experienced all her many moods, but I had never seen her like this before. At first she just stared at me with a hard, determined look on her face; after a few seconds her face softened into the Candi I knew and had come to love, then a great sadness covered her face and I thought far a moment she was going to cry. A second later she threw herself into my arms and held on tight for the better part of a minute before the normal everyday Candi appeared and she acted as though nothing strange had happened.

I tried to think back to the first time I had noticed a change in Candi; it began just after we started to harvest our first plants. When she returned from Honolulu after confirming the deal and getting her up-front money she'd appeared nervous and uneasy. At times she seemed lost in thought and oblivious to everything around her. I attributed her mood swings to the fact that she had just celebrated her thirty-ninth birthday—she'd often said that she would never see her fortieth birthday; I wrote it off to counterculture rhetoric. But I had been unable to shake the feeling that either something was going on I didn't know about or I didn't understand. The feeling had grown to something beyond my usual concerns for Candi.

Also, in the last three months she had spent more time in Honolulu than was normal for her; this, as well as a host of little things to which I would normally have paid little mind, added to my apprehension. There had been many times during the ten years I'd lived with Candi when she had been withdrawn and aloof—sometimes she talked her head off, at other times she went without uttering a single word for a day or two; she pouted when she didn't get her way and sometimes she just sat and watched the ocean for hours on end without ever changing her expression. But the past three weeks had been so vastly different I didn't know what to make of it. It was beginning to worry me. Candi hardly ever asked my opinion about anything and when she did she structured the question in such a way as to solicit the answer or action she wanted—in other words she told me what she wanted in the form of a question. I called it the Southern belle technique. But lately she'd asked questions troubling to me, since it was so unlike Candi to ask a question requiring any thought whatsoever. The first such question, which had turned into a series of questions, took me totally by surprise. "How old do you think you will be when you die?"

I said I planned to live forever and if it appeared that wasn't going to be the case I would cross the bridge when I got to it. Without giving any appearance of having heard my answer she asked, "Do you believe our lives are predetermined?" Questions such as these came at me out of the blue; I never knew what to expect next.

Candi fought many battles within; she was a mystery I knew I would never solve. I suspected she was tormented by the life she had been forced to accept rather than the life of luxury she had inherited as a birthright, the life she still secretly wanted. Her anger at her parents and society in general had grown from the seeds planted by radical counterculture activists in her flower-child days, and was nurtured by the natural rebellion of youth toward their parents and the establishment in general—no matter the time or generation, all youth want to cut their own notch in societal evolution. However, her misplaced anger was both a denial and a defense of the choices that had landed her in the hell she was living when fate threw us together. Some of her anger she reserved for me, inasmuch as I mirrored much of her parents' ideology—capitalism versus socialism, doing what is right versus designer morals, and so forth. Hey, don't get me wrong. Integrity wasn't my strong suit—I grew and sold an illegal substance for a living, I was a thief, I had spent time in prison, used the identity of a dead man, shot a federal agent, and hijacked an airplane, not to mention being an army deserter during a time of war. The biggest difference between us, though—maybe the only difference—was that Candi blamed the establishment for all her troubles. It was the standard counterculture copout that justified the choices she had made, and relieved her of all responsibility for them. And it was those choices that had brought her to the point where taking her life seemed to be the only way out of her self-made hell.. On the other hand, I knew the life I was living was the result of my own doing. The choices I had made along the way were of my own free will; no one had forced or coerced me into any of those decisions. The anger she should have reserved for those who took advantage of her youthful rebellious tendencies to recruit her into the free-love, dope-smoking counterculture movement for their own pleasure and robbed her of the upper-middle-class lifestyle rightfully hers, she had turned inward. There had been a period in her life when she reached such a low that all she could see, when looking up, was the bottom. It was during this point in her life that she considered ending it all with a heroin overdose—she had heard it was a beautiful way to go—but, logic, for once, prevailed and her desire to overcome the devils ruling her life had won out.

I still maintained Candi was a witch and had cast a spell over me, and she may indeed have been a witch. Nevertheless, I went under her spell willingly, with few regrets.

I was lost in thought and did not immediately realize a figure wearing a black wetsuit had emerged from the shadows carrying a bulky wet-proof bag which I assumed was full of hundred-dollar bills. I was wrong.

I recognized the approaching figure as a relative of a local politician known to locals as the Island Godfather. He gave me a wide grin and said, "Hey man, you got some good shit."

"Best in The Islands," I replied. "I trust you've got enough in the bag to cover everything."

"Don't worry about that, old buddy, you gonna get everything you got coming."

I didn't like the way he said, that. There was the hint of a sneer on his face and the way he emphasized "everything you got coming" sent a little chill up my spine. I found myself wishing I hadn't vowed to give up packing heat after shooting the federal agent back in Washington State. One thing was for sure, I wasn't his buddy; I had never liked or trusted the guy and preferred not to do business with him, but he paid top dollar and always showed up as promised. He operated pretty much in the open; the word was being a relative of the Godfather he didn't worry about getting busted.

He walked past me, unzipped the mosquito netting just enough to slip the bag inside and said, "Check this out."

I didn't think much about it at the time; after all, Candi had made the deal.

A faint glow illuminated the tent walls, I assumed Candi was removing and counting bundles of cash from the bag. Again I was wrong.

It was about this time I spotted a second black-clad figure approaching from out of the shadows. He walked unhurriedly and stopped a few feet away opposite his boss. He looked at his boss, then at me, then back at his boss before speaking, "We're loaded, you about finished?"

"Yeah, just some loose ends to tie up." It was at this time that Candi emerged from the tent dressed in a black wetsuit identical to those worn by the two guys standing in front of me—it was then I realized what was in the bag.

I wasn't exactly sure of what was going down, but I knew it was going to end badly for me. My pulse was racing and my mind was processing information at warp speed. The extra shots of adrenaline pumped into my system made things appear in slow motion.

I hadn't noticed the wetsuits were designed with chest pockets until the guy ripped open the Velcro fastener and I caught the glint of stainless steel. It was as though time stood still as my brain processed information provided by my senses and my thoughts. I wasn't thinking about the fact that the guy was going to shoot me down in cold blood. I was listening to a gentle surf move thousands of tiny ocean grinders up and down the beach. In the end they would become sand. I could see the millions of stars in a sky that stretched to the dark edge of the Pacific Ocean. I could feel the soft breeze whispering as it passed through the long, slender needles of the nearby Australian pines and touched my skin as gently as a firelight cast shadow. My only thoughts were of how much I wanted to live.

I still hadn't moved as he withdrew a short-nose thirty-eight Chief's Special and brought it to bear on my chest. It was Candi who broke the spell; she lunged at him screaming, "No!" She knocked him off balance and he fell to his knees as his first shot went wide. Candi continued her attack as she threw herself on top of him, knocking him to the ground as she screamed, "You promised."

Whatever deal Candi had made didn't include my death. She had given me a chance and I took it. I zigzagged as I sprinted for the jungle. I heard bullets singing as they passed close by and slammed against the trees only a few feet ahead of me, followed a microsecond later by the reports of four shots. I knew the Chief's Special held only five rounds and I figured I was safe since I would reach the trees before he could reload. A couple of seconds later more bullets crashed into the trees as the sound of five more shots echoed in the night. Obviously his buddy was packing the same type of weapon. I figured he couldn't see me and was just shooting in the direction I had fled; nevertheless, they were still too close for comfort.

I darted behind the first large tree and peered back toward the beach. There was no moon, but stars provided enough light for me to make out their silhouettes against the ocean. They were still standing by the fire looking toward the spot where I had entered the jungle. I guessed they were discussing whether or not to come looking for me. Several seconds passed before they headed toward the beach and their Zodiac; the guys walked together with Candi following a few steps behind as she scanned the jungle, and I may be mistaken, but I will swear she stopped and blew me a kiss.

A third guy waited by the Zodiac. Candi tossed the waterproof bag she was carrying into the boat and climbed in after it while the three guys pushed the Zodiac off the beach; they jumped inside as soon as it began to float. A few seconds later the powerful outboard motors roared to life and the Zodiac backed out into deeper water. The helmsman kept it slow until clear of the cove and then turning northeast, he opened the throttles on the outboards and in a matter of seconds had the boat riding on the step and skimming across the water toward, I surmised, Honolulu. I was pretty sure no one had remained behind to finish me off; nevertheless, I remained hidden for almost an hour after the sounds of the outboards had faded away.

I walked slowly back to the tent and fumbled around in the dark until I located a mini-Maglite. With the aid of the small flashlight I found and pulled on some heavier clothes along with Gore-Tex pants and jacket—when running at top speed the Grand Raid threw up a lot of spray and although the temperature even this late at night and this time of year was in the 70s, running at 20 knots for an extended period with wet skin was to risk hypothermia. I gathered up my wallet and a few more items, stuffed them inside a waterproof bag, and then headed for the Grand Raid hidden behind the waterfall. I pushed the boat into the water and wasted no time getting the motors started. I powered through the surf where the Pacific Ocean spilled into the cove and turned southwest toward Hilo.

I tied off the Grand Raid in the marina, then walked to the parking lot, pulled a pair of cutoffs, a tank top, and my wallet from the waterproof bag before tossing it onto the passenger seat of the Rusty Bucket. I quickly shucked the Gore-Tex and the rest of my clothing and then slipped on the dry clothes, making sure my wallet was safely secured in a pocket on the cutoffs. Next, I disconnected the boat trailer, cranked up the old Chevy, drove straight to the airport, and purchased a ticket on the first flight to Honolulu. There wasn't anything I needed in Pahoa Town and I had no further use for the boat and trailer or the Rusty Bucket. I had wanted out of the marijuana trade and now I was out. This wasn't the way I had planned to retire, but nevertheless, I was out and I intended to stay out. I also figured if I wanted to die of old age it would behoove me to get as far away from The Islands as I could as fast as I could. As it turned out, getting out of Hawaii wasn't that easy.

It was late afternoon before I deplaned in Honolulu and by the time the taxi dropped me on Fort Street, banks were already closed. I hit up the ATM for the maximum amount I could withdraw, walked up to Chinatown, and found a room for the night. I doubted anyone would be looking for me, but why take the chance. I paid in cash and signed in under an alias. "You like girl?" the old woman at the desk asked.

That was the last thing on my mind, but I wanted to blend in, so I said, "Later."

"I send pretty girl, you like her." The old woman handed me a key and directed me to my room. Less than an hour passed and I had just finished my shower and crawled into bed when there was a soft knock at the door. I let her in; she was pretty, just as the old woman promised. We discussed her fee before I asked, "If I pay double will you come back in the morning?"

"You no like me?" she asked.

"Yes, I'm very attracted to you, but I'm tired and I will enjoy you more after a good night's rest." Her eyes brightened and a smile replaced the frown when I counted out two hundred dollars and pushed the bills toward her. She reached for the money and said, "Okay, I come back. Eight o'clock?"

"That will be fine." Whether or not she would be back I didn't know. It didn't matter; I would be gone by six.

I awoke hungry. Except for the container of shrimp-fried rice I had purchased in Chinatown before checking into the hotel I hadn't eaten in more than thirty-six hours, so I took a taxi to Perry's Smorgasbord on Kuhio Street and satiated my appetite. I figured it would be safer for me to not just leave Hawaii but to get completely out of the country, so I decided to visit my ex-wife's family in the Philippines. I had no reason to believe anyone would come looking for me, but it seemed like a good time to heed the old axiom, "Better safe than sorry." At the bank I retrieved my passport and ten thousand dollars from Candi's safe-deposit box—I was surprised the money was still there. The safe-deposit box was in both our names, but Candi considered it hers and referred to it as hers. From Fort Street I took a taxi to the Philippine embassy and applied for a visa. I was told it would take forty-eight hours. It would be available for pickup anytime after noon on the third day.

Although my ex-wife's parents were deceased, their home had passed on to the oldest son, who still lived in the house with his wife and two sons. He got in touch with his younger sister, who invited me to move in with her, which I did. It didn't take long for me to realize I had entered into another unworkable arrangement.

My ex-wife, according to her sister, was dead; the family had been unable to find out exactly what happened, but it appeared to have something to do with drugs and prostitution. Little sister made it quite clear she was willing to take up where her big sister had left off—she too wanted a ticket to America. It didn't take long for me to realize there was nothing for me in the PI and before I knew it I found myself back on Oahu.

I checked with my management company and found I had a fully furnished one-bedroom condo on the thirty-second floor of Canterbury Place available—this was a unit my management company rented to Japanese tourists on an extended visit to Hawaii. With the Japanese economy flying high, a week in Hawaii was cheaper than a night out in Tokyo. Since I had incorporated shortly after my holdings began to grow, there was no easy way to trace anything directly to me and no reason for anyone to suspect I would be living in a penthouse in one of newest condominiums in Waikiki. I felt safe for the moment.

Whether it was a secret yearning to reunite with Candi or the desire for revenge that brought me back to Hawaii I really can't say; perhaps it was just fate. Whatever the reason may have been, I now had time on my hands and spending time alone makes for loneliness. I often found myself thinking about Candi and the good times we'd known and at night she dominated my dreams. I found myself wondering, was she a witch after all and was I still under her spell? It didn't matter. I knew she would never again be part of my life and I was better off without her.

Having time on my hands required that I find new interests or go crazy from boredom. I started reading the newspaper and watching the news and realized I knew nothing about things affecting the economy. I was familiar with the terms *inflation* and *cost of living index*, but in reality they meant nothing to me. I quickly understood how they affected the market, my everyday life, and how they would affect my future—my real estate investments had been making money due to inflation and I didn't even know it. It was time to plan for the future. I asked my broker to send me a list of all my holdings and in order to gain some small understanding of the market I subscribed to several financial newsletters—all my mail went to my broker.

As another ploy to kill time, I began writing my memoirs, as Candi had suggested when we first arrived in The Islands. I spent a few minutes every day writing down things I recalled from my past. It was during one of these sessions about two months after I arrived back in Hawaii that I received a call from my broker. "I just signed for a registered letter addressed to you. You might want to come by and pick it up, it could be important."

I recognized the handwriting on the envelope immediately. A tinge of excitement raced through my entire being—I wanted to read the letter in absolute privacy, so I headed back to Canterbury Place. Candi knew our bank statements were sent to an address in Honolulu—I had told her it was a mail collection agency and she believed me; she had no reason to think otherwise. She was unaware it was the address of my broker, who received all my mail, including bank statements. She knew nothing about the fact that all bills for property taxes, insurance premiums, homeowners associations, and a host of maintenance and cleaning bills, an integral part of turning a profit when owning rental property, were forwarded to my broker as well, which he paid out of my accounts. His accountant prepared my federal and state income tax returns. His fee for services was probably a little high, but it was well worth it to me.

My excitement grew and by the time I reached the thirty-second floor of Canterbury Place I was almost delirious. My hands were shaking as I sat down and opened the letter. I was prepared for anything except the letter inside. I slumped down in my chair; the letter fell to the floor as I wiped away tears and half-whispered, "Such a waste."

I repeated the statement several more times before I finally got up, walked into the bathroom, and washed my face and dried my eyes. Having recovered from the initial shock I picked up and reread the letter.

> My dearest DB,
>
> Do you remember the night we met? I do. I think of it often, more so recently. You stole my heart with the story about how your mother named you DB. Although you've used other names since then, I will always remember you as DB.
>
> You must think badly of me. I hope you don't. I've been dishonest with you in so many ways, but I have loved you since the moment I looked into your eyes for the first time. I know you have deceived me as well. I also know you did it for my own good, but still, as hard as you tried, you were unable to protect me from myself. You were right all along; I threw away the dreams of my youth just as I threw away the life I had with you—you were the best thing that happened to me since I ran away from La Jolla.
>
> I know you didn't believe me, although I tried to tell you several times I would die young. I have always known I would never live past forty; it was my destiny. Perhaps it was

nothing more than a self-created prophecy, I don't know, but I do know it has come to pass. Yes, by the time you read this letter I will be at peace, my destiny fulfilled.

Believing, as I did, that my life was limited and with time running out, I wanted desperately to have one year of luxury. I wanted to cram all the things I could have had, but didn't have, and the things I could have done, but never did into one year. That was what I was promised; that wasn't what I got. I was also promised you wouldn't be harmed and you would be paid for your crop; that night on the beach was just the beginning of a long string of broken promises.

It doesn't matter now; the only thing that matters to me is that you are alive and well and for you to know I never stopped loving you. Your face is the last image my mind will let me see; I will carry it with me into eternity.

Live long and be happy, D.B. Cooper, and if you are ever lonely, I hope you will think of me and the good times we shared.

You were my hero,
Candi

I remembered seeing in the news and reading in the morning paper about a woman's body being found in Ala Moana Park. The autopsy indicated she had died from a drug overdose. Authorities were asking for help in identifying her. I took a stiff drink of Wild Turkey to help steady my nerves before retrieving the *Honolulu Advertiser* from the trash and reading the entire piece—I had read only the headlines before. The description fit. With the help of another shot of whiskey I picked up the phone and called the number listed in the paper. I was given the address of the city morgue and who to ask for once I arrived.

I stopped by the bank and took Candi's passport and our marriage certificate from her safe-deposit box and slipped them along with Candi's letter inside the envelope I'd picked up from the teller who let me into the vault. I figured the letter in her handwriting and the postmarked envelope would put an end to any investigation that might be underway—I didn't want an investigation; an inquiry into my life could lead into areas best left alone.

I wasn't looking forward to identifying the body, but it was less difficult than I anticipated. She appeared to be sleeping and, even in death, was as beautiful as ever. I wanted to believe, just as she said in her letter, my face was the last thing she saw and the smile on her lips was for me.

The authorities were eager to wrap up the case and bought my story hook, line, and sinker. Entries in my passport backed up the separation story I fed them.

The gravity of the situation finally hit when I was asked, "What arrangements would you like to make for interment?"

It was a routine question necessary to finalize the case. The detective had asked it many times before in similar situations, but he realized it was not easy for me and excused himself from the room. He returned a few minutes later and presented me with a cardboard file box. "The only things found on her were these two rings and her clothes; you may take them with you."

He handed me a small plastic Ziploc bag containing the rings I had stolen from the house in Vancouver, Washington. We had used the rings during the short ceremony in front of a justice of the peace when we were married. In the box was the outfit I had bought her at El Paso Saddle and Blanket Company. I was on the verge of losing what little composure I had left. The detective knew the tears weren't fake and excused himself again. He returned in due time with a handful of forms and pamphlets explaining my options. Although I was under no obligation to accept responsibility, I decided to have Candi cremated with the rings on her finger and in the clothes she was wearing when she died. I figured if she chose to wear the western outfit to her death she would be content wearing it in eternity.

For the next couple of weeks I left Canterbury Place only for food and whiskey; during the day I watched television and wrote about my life's experiences, at night I got drunk and planned my revenge. I wanted the son-of-a-bitch to know why he was dying and by whose hand. My decision made, I poured what booze I had left down the drain and vowed not to touch another drink until the SOB occupied his own slab in the morgue or better yet, was never heard from again.

I hadn't shaved or cut my hair since the day I'd brought Candi's ashes home from the crematorium. I don't know why, probably it was because I was drunk most of the time. Whatever the reason, I figured it would be to my advantage to continue growing a beard. It would make it less likely anyone would recognize me.

For several months I watched my quarry until I knew everything about him, his every habit. I knew where he lived, what cars he drove, places he frequented, when he ate, and when he slept and with whom.

I committed to memory the faces of his pushers, where and when they met, how he arranged drops and picked up cash. No matter the time of day or night, I could tell you where he was and what he was doing with 90 percent accuracy. I was ready; it was time.

He was big on running and ran for an hour almost daily in Kapiolani Park. I started running again. I was in pretty good shape from transporting supplies up and marijuana down cliffs on the Big Island. And it hadn't been that long ago that, as part of my training for Operation Quick Rich, I was running 20 miles a day with a 30-pound backpack in two and a half hours and not even breathing hard and sometimes barely breaking a sweat. Within a month I was running a seven-minute mile.

Candi's killer ran religiously at five o'clock in the morning, I ran at five in the morning—he may not have slipped the needle into her vein but nevertheless he was instrumental in her death; as far as I was concerned he killed her. Most runners tank up on water, Gatorade, or some other energy drink before departing on their run, and they are aware of water stops along the way. This usually requires a pit stop for anyone running for an hour or more; everybody has a favorite pit stop.

I paced him step for step, making sure to stay about fifteen seconds ahead, and making sure no one was between us. I hit the pit stop and pretended to be shaking it off when he entered. The guy was also into martial arts and I knew I would have to act first and talk later. I pulled up my sweatpants and turned as though to exit. As we were about to pass I stepped into his path and drove the knife deep into the soft tissue just below the ribcage. Without withdrawing the knife I adjusted the angle several times and with each adjustment I forced the 8-inch blade of a double-edged Gerber up into his vital organs with all the strength I could muster, driving the blade deeper with each thrust. When I finally withdrew the knife and took a step back I looked him in the eyes and said, "Remember me, old buddy?" I put special emphasis on the words *old buddy*. He was still standing, looking at me in disbelief, his face a ghostly white, when I said, "That was for Candi." He made a futile attempt to lunge at me and fell to his hands and knees. I stepped forward, reached down, grabbed a handful of hair, yanked his head up, and then slit his throat as I whispered in his ear, "And that's for me, you backstabbing son-of-a-bitch."

I was amazed at how little blood there was on me, but there was enough to indisputably link me to his death should I be apprehended. I stripped down to my running shorts and tied the sweats around my waist as runners often do after overheating. I continued on my route until I reached Queen's Beach. I walked into to the ocean, then swam out into the surf for perhaps a hundred yards and dropped the knife, my sweats, and my shoes and socks—any blood splatters on my body were washed clean. I continued to swim parallel to the beach until I reached Fort Derussy and then ran along the beach until I reached the Hilton. I walked past their pool and cut through the gardens and past numerous gift shops and boutiques until I reached Ala Moana Boulevard. From there it was a short walk to Canterbury Place.

Anticipating success in extracting my revenge I'd bought hair clippers at a local pawnshop; I used the hair clippers to cut off my beard before scraping off what remained with a throwaway razor—the aftershave stung but my face felt smooth and soft. I used the hair clippers to give myself a close military-style haircut, which to my surprise looked pretty good. The clippers, razor, hair, beard, aftershave, along with all personal items I wasn't taking with me went into the trash. My bags were already packed. The clothes I would be wearing when I left The Islands for the last time were hanging in the closet. The clothes I would wear until then lay on the bureau. I had already informed my broker I would be leaving The Islands soon and would call before I left. My flight would be leaving for Dallas, Texas just after midnight; from there I would take a bus to Houston—I didn't believe the precautions to cover my tracks were necessary, but I was still adhering to the old adage, *Better safe than sorry*. For old times' sake, I walked down to Perry's on Lewers and ate breakfast with a ghost, but I was calm and relaxed, which surprised me. I was holding up well. After breakfast I walked back up to the bus stop on Kalia Road and caught the Number 19 to a stop near Fort Street. The bank had been open only a few minutes when a teller let me into the vault and retrieved Candi's safe-deposit box. I followed her to a private booth where she placed the box on a small table, and said, "Call me when you're finished."

I transferred all the cash to a leather valise. I had taken only ten thousand dollars the day after fleeing the Big Island. I thought there was a possibility Candi would change her mind and need the money for her own escape. Nevertheless, when I retrieved Candi's passport and our marriage certificate in preparation for identifying her for the authorities, the money was still there. I could only speculate as to why she hadn't removed it. The teller handed me the key after locking the box back in its little space in the vault. I thanked her and left. At a bank across the street I cleaned out four safe-deposit boxes Candi knew nothing about. The first box was nearly full of gold coins. On 31 December 1974 President Gerald Ford signed into law the right for private citizens to own gold. Between then and July, 1978, when gold hit two hundred dollars an ounce, I bought as many gold coins as I could afford. More than half were American eagles and double eagles, the rest were South African krugerrandands and Austrian coronas. I dumped the gold coins and the contents from the other three boxes into the valise. I had to stuff two bundles of hundred-dollar bills into my pockets before the valise would close and lock. I double checked the locks before calling the teller.

Back at Canterbury Place I called my broker and informed him I would be leaving the following day. Next I arranged for a taxi to pick me up at ten thirty. I didn't want to be late checking in, neither did I want to show up too early—I wanted as little exposure as possible. I set my two alarm clocks for six, pulled off my clothes and added them to the trash, then climbed into bed and fell asleep—I slept long and well; there were no nightmares to wake me.

Cobwebs and Dust

I deplaned in Dallas amongst a lot of disgruntled passengers; a storm had held up all incoming and departing flights for about six hours. The airport had been open to traffic for only about thirty minutes when I arrived. I'd been having second thoughts about taking a bus to Houston—too many people of questionable character hung out around bus stations. I decided the quickest and easiest way out of the airport and Dallas was to rent a car and drive to Houston. To my way of thinking, although their one-way drop-off fee was excessive, the service was convenient and the only logical choice. In less than an hour after walking up to a Hertz kiosk I was sitting in a Cadillac Deville on Interstate 45 with Dallas in the rearview mirror.

It was well after dark when I reached the outskirts of Houston. I spotted a Holiday Inn located a couple of blocks off the freeway and since I was both tired and hungry, figured this would be a good place to settle in for the night. The off-ramp merged into a street with several fast-food joints. I spotted a McDonald's, pulled into their drive-through lane and ordered two Big Macs and a double order of fries, and then pulled up to the window and waited. Within a couple of minutes a girl opened the window and repeated my order back to me and said, "That'll be four dollars and twenty-nine cents, please."

I handed her a five-dollar bill and said, "Keep the change."

She smiled as she passed me my food and said, "Thank you, have a nice evening."

I asked for a ground-level room and backed into the parking space directly in front of the door. I tossed my luggage onto the bed closest to the door before locking the car. Back inside my room I closed and locked the door and then slipped the safety chain in place before opening a cabinet underneath the bathroom sink and handcuffing the valise to a water pipe—a precaution that was no doubt unnecessary. I turned on the TV and switched the channel to CNN, and then pulled the bedspread off the bed farthest from the door and let it drop to the floor at the foot of the bed. I kicked off my shoes and hung my clothes in the closet before crawling into bed. I propped my head up on a couple of pillows and watched the news while eating my supper. There was nothing about a stabbing death in Waikiki. I doubted it would make the national news—Hawaii's Visitor's Bureau wouldn't want to scare off tourists.

Having done a lot of biking in my earlier years, I was one of those guys with *Easy Rider* aspirations, but I was too old to start wandering about the country on a motorcycle while living out of a sea bag. So I located the guy who'd bought our RV in the early '70s.

"Remember me?" I asked.

He looked me over for several seconds before replying. "No, can't say that I do."

"I sold you a motor home about ten years ago; you paid me in cash and called me a taxi so I could get to the airport."

He looked at me for a few more seconds and started patting his forehead with the palm of his hand and then with a big grin he pointed his finger at me, moving it back and forth a few times. "Yeah, now I remember, you had that foxy chick with you."

I wasn't aware I let any emotion show, but he picked up on something and quickly said, "I didn't mean to offend, but she's the kind of woman you don't forget."

"No offence taken, and you're right, she is the kind of woman you don't forget." I unconsciously referred to Candi in the present tense; it was difficult to think of her any other way.

"Okay, so what can I do for you today?"

His operation had doubled several times over since I'd sold him the motor home. He had hundreds of RVs on his lot, some used, but mostly new. "I need your help; I'm ready to buy an RV but I don't know what would serve my needs best and I'm trusting you to give me good advice and treat me right."

"I'll do just that, I'll treat you right and give you my best advice. What price range do you have in mind?"

"The price is not a problem; however, when I turn the key I want it to start and I don't want to be stopping at every town I pass through to have something repaired."

He looked at me for a few seconds, "Have you had lunch?"

"No sir."

"Well, I think a lot better on a full stomach, let's get something to eat."

I followed him out of his office into an enormous showroom where several RVs were set up, some with awnings out and one with a Florida room attached. He spoke briefly to one of the salesmen.

"What kind of food would you like?"

"Well, I'm a Texas boy and I've been out of the state for a while."

He broke in before I could finish.

"So you're looking for some Tex-Mex." I grinned and nodded.

"Come on, I know just the place."

A waitress took our order while a busboy placed salsa, corn chips, and water on the table. Both quickly departed. I had a slight suspicion I might be getting hustled. As though reading my mind he said, "Contrary to what some people think, I'm an honest businessman. I freely admit, I'm in business to make money, but you can't build a business the size of mine and have as many repeat customers as I do by cheating people. You find a legitimate deal better than the one I make you and I'll match it and throw in an extra five hundred dollars"

Perhaps my first impression of the guy when I sold him my motor home had been wrong. I nodded and said, "I like to believe in people until they prove I can't trust them, and I have no reason to think you aren't being honest with me."

"Thank you; now tell me how you intend to use your RV. Will you be on the road most of the time, will you stay in commercial parks or in the boonies, how many people will travel with you?" Before he could ask another question we were interrupted by the waitress as she placed our food on the table.

"Wow, this looks good, do you mind if I eat and talk at the same time?"

The guy's face crinkled as he laughed and said, "That's what I had in mind."

I waded into my meal for several minutes before slowing down enough to talk; I gestured to the food as I said, "Muy bueno." I continued before he could speak. "Okay, I want something large enough to be comfortable for one or two people, but small enough to make it easily maneuverable. I probably won't stay in commercial parks very often, but again I might, but number one is stability and reliability."

"I have two, maybe three models of high-end motor coaches I recommend. You will be happy with either of them. I'll explain the advantages and disadvantages when I show them to you."

We took our time finishing lunch as he explained some of the dos and don'ts of RVing. Over churros and coffee the RV dealer started to speak, hesitated, and then said. "I sell RVs, not cars, but you may want to consider towing a small vehicle. I'm not trying to hustle you, but you asked for my advice." He continued to lay out the advantages and disadvantages of towing another vehicle.

"If you're interested, and again I'm not trying to push something off on you, I took a Holiday Rambler in on a trade last week complete with a Chevrolet Cavalier on a custom-made trailer. I'll sell you the car and trailer for low book. Like I said, I sell RVs, not automobiles, and I'm interested in getting it off my lot."

The first RV he showed me was the one I bought along with the car and trailer. He referred to the motor home as a "class A basement-model diesel pusher."

"Since you paid me in cash I think it only fair I return the favor, is that okay with you?"

"Cash always works for me, and since you're paying in cash I'll personally take the paperwork over to DMV this afternoon and get it registered for you and have the Cavalier transferred to your name. By this time day after tomorrow I'll have both vehicles washed and serviced with a full fuel tank and ready for the road." He hesitated for a few seconds and then continued cautiously and in a slightly more serious tone.

"I will be required to show proof of liability insurance in your name for both vehicles before the Department of Motor Vehicles will register them. They also require an instate address and a Texas driver's license. Since I have an agent who writes insurance policies for me I can help you out with the first part. As far as the address and driver's license goes, you are on your own, but I'll need all three before I can register the vehicles for you. You can take care of all the paperwork yourself, but it will be a lot easier for you if I take care of everything—they know me and know I'm legit."

Since my real estate holdings and the bank accounts in El Paso were in my real name I'd been giving serious thought to the idea of taking up my birth name again. I figured since Jimmy Carter had pardoned all the draft dodgers the Feds had no interest in pursuing the desertion warrant, providing they had ever issued one, and stopped looking for me a long time ago—if by chance they were still looking for me and I was arrested I would claim I enlisted under pressure of an El Paso judge. So I gave him my father's west Texas address and told him I would stop by the local Division of Motor Vehicles and get a driver's license. I followed his directions to the nearest DMV office, studied their handout booklet for about thirty minutes and left with a brand-new Texas driver's license. I stopped back by the RV dealership, where a girl photocopied both sides of my newly acquired driver's license, while I signed all the paperwork. I paid for the insurance, and was instructed to call the following day.

I found a motel nearby and watched television most of the afternoon. By eight o'clock I was hungry and called a local pizza delivery joint. The following morning I took advantage of the motel's continental breakfast bar before calling the RV dealership. I was told I could take possession of the vehicles any time after noon on the following day. I spent the rest of the day in my room, ordered out for dinner, and hit the motel's breakfast bar again the next morning. After calling Hertz for directions to their closest drop-off point, I stayed in my room until a few minutes before the mandatory checkout time. I took a taxi from the Hertz return lot to the RV dealership. Just as promised, my rig was sitting out in front of the showroom all shiny and ready to go.

The owner was there to personally hand me the keys. "If this *bad boy* gives you any problems bring him back and I'll make it right, okay?"

"Okay." We shook hands, thanked each other and I was on my way—to where, I didn't know.

I pulled into the parking lot at a *Wally World* superstore and transferred all the money and gold coins in the valise, except for two thousand dollars, to the fireproof lockbox hidden behind a panel in the kitchen. On the way into the store I dropped the valise into a trash can. I spent almost eight hundred dollars on cooking utensils, dishes, flatware, plastic storage containers, food, and a few other things I though might come in handy.

On Interstate 10 about halfway between Houston and San Antonio I pulled into a rest stop on the truckers' side and hit the switch for the automatic leveling jacks, fired up the auxiliary generator, turned on the TV, adjusted the rooftop satellite dish, and channeled to CNN—after two weeks of checking the news every day without any mention of a stabbing death on Oahu I figured I didn't need to be overly concerned about where the authorities were looking.

It was a month later that I checked into the Chula Vista Kampgrounds of America (KOA) just off Second Avenue. There was only one thing I had to do in San Diego and it required taking a chance. I had no reason to take the chance, but I believed it was one way of helping me shake the cobwebs and dust of the past from my mind.

It was a few minutes past sundown when I left the Cavalier at Lindbergh Field and rented a one-way drop-off car to Los Angeles. I drove back to the KOA, where I retrieved a shopping bag from the motor home and placed it on the passenger's seat. The bag was the type used by upscale department stores when you've purchased an expensive item. I was careful to touch only the little rope handles; I'd already cleaned the bag and the urn inside to insure that all fingerprints were removed. I returned to the motor coach, stripped off my clothes, and pulled on a pair of khaki pants and a burgundy turtleneck, stepped into a pair of loafers, and then slipped on a navy blazer. I checked to make sure the item I had placed in the inside pocket of the blazer earlier in the day was still there. There was no reason it shouldn't have been, but I double-checked just the same.

My emotions ran high as I drove along the street in La Jolla, near Bird Rock, where, almost ten years before, I had watched Candi slowly turn her head as we drove past the house I surmised to be her childhood home—it was the only time I ever saw her cry. I parked by the privacy fence in front of the house, walked up to the front door, set the shopping bag on the porch, and rang the bell. I wasn't absolutely sure I had the right house until the door opened. I sucked in my breath at the sight of the woman standing in front of me. There was no need to ask the question. Except for the way she wore her hair, it was Candi. The lady was eighteen to twenty years older, but there was no doubt in my mind—this was Candi's mother. I asked the question just the same.

I removed the passport from the inside pocket of my jacket and slipped the baggie back so as to expose one end without actually touching the small blue booklet. I extended my arm toward the lady, holding the passport within easy reach. "Ma'am, is this your daughter?"

The lady's quick intake of breath when she opened the passport left no doubt I was indeed looking at Candi's mother. I had cut out the passport number, as well as the name and address, but the picture and stamped pages were intact. The lady turned and called to her husband, then returned her attention to me. She slowly looked me up and down. Her husband joined her just as she asked, "Do you know my daughter?"

"Yes ma'am. I knew her well; we were married ten years ago." I didn't want to get into a long conversation; I wanted to get it over with and get out of there as quickly as possible. I was having second thoughts, but I'd gone too far to back out, so I continued without giving either of her parents a chance to ask a question.

"This is very difficult for me and I know it is going to be difficult for you as well." I hesitated for only a moment before continuing.

"Your daughter loved you very much and spoke of you often. She wanted you to know how much she regretted running away from home and how she wished she'd had the courage to stay after you brought her home from Juneau. I tried to persuade her to come and visit with you or at least call and let you know she was well and happy, but she was afraid the old adage 'You can never go home' was true. We did drive by your house once, but she wouldn't let me stop. Whatever her feelings may have been, her last request was, and she made me swear, I would bring her home."

Okay, so I was lying, but then again, maybe not. I believe Candi really did love her parents and wished she hadn't run away from home, but would not admit it except to herself. However that might be, I could see no reason to hurt her parents further. Candi had already caused them enough grief, so I fabricated a story I hoped would give them some solace and put to rest any questions about their daughter's life and how she came to her end.

I picked up the shopping bag with both hands; one on each of the little rope handles, so it was open at the top and held it out toward Candi's father. They looked at each other and then back at me before her father lifted the urn from the bag. I thought Candi's mother might faint; her knees began to sag as she leaned against her husband, and he slipped his arm around her waist for support. No one said anything for what seemed like an eternity; Candi's mother had both arms around her husband, her face buried against his shoulder; her sobbing was soft but audible. He set the urn aside and wrapped both arms around his wife and held her tight.

I was about to leave when she turned to face me, tears were streaming down her face, and her voice was barely audible when she asked, "What happened to her?"

"Leukemia, ma'am. It was in its final stage before the doctors figured out why she ran out of energy every day. She refused treatment, preferring to stay home. Near the end we employed a live-in nurse to care for her. She was never in pain." She dabbed her eyes with the handkerchief her husband placed in her hand.

"Earlier you alluded to her happiness—was she happy?"

"From the moment we met until her last breath we were both very happy. As you can see from her passport we traveled extensively, we had a great ten years. I made sure she never wanted for anything."

"Would you like to come inside and visit with us for a while?"

"Thank you, but I doubt it would benefit either of us. Although I will never forget your daughter I prefer to grieve in private. I hope someday to get past the pain. It was hard enough for me to come and tell you these things. But to sit across from you, a spitting image of your daughter, and relive the memories I have of her and have you tell me about her childhood would be more than I care to endure. I wish you well."

I turned and walked away without offering my hand or looking back. I was reaching for the gate when I heard the door close.

There was probably no need to take precautions to cover my tracks—nevertheless, I dropped off the rental car at LAX and caught the next flight back to San Diego, picked up the Cavalier and drove back to KOA.

Having slept well, I was up early the next morning. I knew I would never be free of the past but my load seemed a lot lighter. I could have spread Candi's ashes in the surf with the same result, and achieved the same end for myself, but putting things to rest for her parents was just as important.

The spring rains were at midseason in southern California, so I moved my rig to the desert and started working on my memoirs again. It occupied my mind for a while, but I soon became bored with nothing to do during the day other than hike and sitting around a campfire at night talking with other RVers, or looking through their telescopes at distant constellations. It wasn't that I missed Candi, which I did; it was the aloneness waiting to engulf me when I returned to my rig at night. I was beginning to think *Easy Rider* wasn't all it was cracked up to be.

I decided to seek out historical sites around the country; at least this would give me something to look forward to from one day to the next. I drove into Yuma and purchased several travel books for RVers before checking into one of the numerous RV parks—it appeared to me Yuma was the snowbird capital of the West. However, most were heading north for the summer and finding a place to stay was not a problem. Finding a spot in the middle of winter is next to impossible, or so I was told.

I've heard it is said, sooner or later everyone returns to the scene of their crime. So, it was probably more than coincidence that I was perusing a list of places to see and things to do in Washington State when I came across an article that jumped right off the page. "D. B. Cooper Days—Cowlitz County invites you to join us in Ariel, Washington; for live music, dancing, local arts and crafts, a chili cook-off, and featuring the famous D. B. Cooper look-alike contest."

How could I ignore a D. B. Cooper look-alike contest? Was fate calling to me or was I on the verge of daring fate? My interest piqued,

I nosed the motor coach northward. There was no need to hurry; November was six months away.

The distance I traveled on any particular day was unimportant since I had everything I needed close at hand in my condominium on wheels. It was just past noon; lunch and a siesta seemed in order, so I pulled into a rest stop on Interstate 15 somewhere north of Cedar City, Utah. I shut the engine down just as the passenger's door of an eighteen-wheeler parked next to me flew open and a shapely woman of about thirty-five exited in unladylike fashion. She had barely picked herself up off the pavement when an open suitcase, a rather large purse, and a guitar in a hardcover carrying case followed her. The guitar came to a rest beside her clothes which landed in an untidy heap. A hand reached out and closed the door; seconds later the big rig began rolling and headed for the Interstate. The woman was yelling something and making hand gestures in the direction of the departing truck and trailer as she picked up her clothes and stuffed them back into the suitcase.

In addition to the standard door about a third of the way back on the passenger side, my motor home had a door allowing the driver to exit directly from the driver's seat. The woman was just closing her suitcase when I opened my door and climbed down within 3 feet of her. She didn't miss a beat. She picked herself up, hefted her suitcase with one hand while holding the guitar and purse in the other, looked me over for about five seconds, and then in a sweet little voice one might have mistaken for a twelve-year-old girl's asked, "Would you take me home?"

"I don't know, maybe. Where do you live?"

"I don't mean my home, I mean, would you take me home with you?"

It was my turn to look her over; I took my time. She was no more than an inch over 5 feet tall with short blonde hair, grey-green eyes, and a nice smile. She was well groomed and the way her Calvin Klein jeans fit I figured she didn't weigh much over a 100 pounds. Her Bally loafers, Christina Dior blazer, Gucci purse, and diamond-studded earrings told me she wasn't some leftover hippie or the average runaway. She would probably cause me grief—what woman hadn't—but I figured it would be a lot better than traveling around the country by myself, and said to no one in particular, "What the hell."

I waved a hand at my rig and said, "*This is* my home."

She looked at my motor coach for a couple of seconds before saying, "It works for me."

I showed her a few of the motor home's features and mentioned a few dos and don'ts associated with RVing. "I pulled into the rest stop because I was getting hungry; have you had lunch?"

"No, I haven't even had breakfast. If you'll point me in the right direction I'll have something ready in a jiffy." Since I intended to fix lunch myself, I reassessed the *Easy Rider* lifestyle and thought perhaps it might not be that bad after all.

Within fifteen minutes she had a couple of grilled ham and cheese sandwiches and two bowls of tomato soup on the table. We were about halfway through the meal before I asked, "What happened with the trucker?"

"You know the story, put out or get out."

"So, you don't put out?"

"Oh, come on, I don't put out to fat slobs with a three-day stubble who smell like they slept in a urinal. He agreed to take me to Salt Lake City, no strings attached, but I had barely climbed into the cab before he demanded we get into the sleeper; I said no and ended up getting physically thrown out of his truck."

"Do you live in Salt Lake?"

"No, and I hadn't given much thought as to what I might do there, perhaps find a job, but mostly I needed to get out of Las Vegas. My husband, a real estate broker, and I moved to Vegas about a year ago. Last month, after twelve years of marriage, he ditched me for a stripper. I didn't take it well and before I knew it I had thrown away most of my settlement on gambling, drinking, and partying. I figured I'd better get out of town while I still had a few dollars and a little dignity left."

"So, how'd you get this far out of Vegas?"

"Did you notice a Plymouth Duster pulled off to the side of the road as you enter the rest stop?"

"The yellow one with its hood up?"

"That's it. I noticed a little red light on the dashboard about 20 miles back. Within a few miles it started getting hot and a knocking sound in the engine grew louder with every mile. Just as I turned into the rest stop there was an explosion inside the engine compartment, it stopped running, and for better or worse—here I am."

When we finished lunch she cleaned up the table, washed the dishes, put them away, and then kicked off her loafers, pulled off her jeans and shirt exposing elegant lingerie with little lace bows, the signature of Bali. Removing her clothes unleashed the delicate aroma of tiny Himalayan roses as the soft fragrance of Joy perfume floated delicately about the coach. She climbed onto the bed, and said, "I could use a nap; how about you?"

Yes indeed, the *Easy Rider* lifestyle just might turn out to be exactly what I had imagined it to be, or at least hoped it to be; whichever, life on the road had just improved 1000 percent from yesterday.

A couple of hours later we fell asleep and it was well after dark before we awoke; an hour or so later Sue Ann, who was indeed blonde, got out of bed and started putting dinner together. Life was good.

We talked about growing up. I told the truth up to a point; whether or not she was truthful I didn't know and didn't care. She had grown up in a small town in Kentucky's Appalachia and was into country music by the time she was ten, got married just out of college and never went back home. Her husband made a lot of money in real estate and things had gone well until they moved to Las Vegas. She was easy to talk with and I told her about my plans for living on the road, and in turn she said getting away from city life would probably heal a lot of wounds and perhaps reintroduce her to her country-girl roots. She asked if she could hang out with me for a while and added with a smile, "I'm a low-maintenance kind of girl." We laid down a few ground rules and everything appeared to be going well, at least for the day—I'd concern myself with tomorrow when and if it arrived.

Sue Ann took to RVing the way a duck takes to water. During the day we'd hike, shop, or sightsee according to our environment and our mood. Sometimes we spent the day just being lazy and lounging around. In the evening she often sat under the motor home's awning in a commercial park or by a fire ring in a backcountry campground and strummed her Martin flat-top guitar. Before long she'd have an audience and often another picker or two would show up with a guitar, banjo, fiddle, or harmonica. Sue Ann's style was reminiscent of Loretta Lynn, but her voice betrayed her idol, Patsy Kline. Sometimes the sessions didn't wind down until midnight, but no one ever complained. I was amazed at how country music could bring complete strangers together and within minutes have them interacting as if they'd known each other all their lives. It felt good just being a part of it.

With only one destination and timeframe in mind I was in no particular hurry but kept moving in a northwesterly direction. A few days here, a week there, and by the end of September we reached the coast and were traveling north on Highway 101. We continued up and around the Olympic Peninsula and by the middle of November I was exactly where I wanted to be—Tacoma, Washington. Why did I want to be in Tacoma? I really didn't know, but I suspect it had something to do with revisiting memories from a particular place and time. A recounting of events that shaped and set in motion a life from which I thought I'd never escape. Perhaps I was trying to cleanse my soul by depositing the baggage I'd picked up along the way back where I found it.

It was late in the evening when I checked into a commercial park. After stabilizing the motor coach, I hooked up to city water, sewer, and electricity and then opened the shut-off valves to my holding tanks. I released the hold-down clamps on the Cavalier, unlocked the tilting mechanism which allowed me to back the little Chevy off the trailer, and parked it in front of the motor home. We were both tired and after a light dinner we took advantage of not having to minimize the use of water and took long hot showers before going to bed early.

I slept late and awoke to the smell of sizzling bacon and hot coffee. After breakfast we took a quick shower, dressed, and headed out for a day of sightseeing. I took Sue Ann to the Bavarian-style town of Leavenworth, where we ate lunch and wandered through arts and craft shows and enjoyed local entertainers. The next day I drove by the area where Candi's old trailer park had stood. A series of commercial warehouses and storage units had replaced the trailer park; there was no evidence it ever existed. The bar where I'd met Candi was still in business, but looked more run down than I remembered, if that were possible.

Finished with my tour, I drove up to Seattle and we spent the rest of the day at Pike Place Market, and had a late dinner before driving back to Tacoma and the comfort and privacy of the motor home. We didn't venture out for the next couple of days. On the third day we drove the Cavalier to Woodland, where I was lucky enough to find a commercial RV park with a space available for six days. I filled in the registration card and paid before asking about the coming weekend festivities in Ariel. The lady handed me a brochure. Across the front it read, D. B. Cooper Days; I smiled and thanked her. We drove back to Tacoma, where I secured the little Chevy on its trailer; all I had left to do was close the holding-tank shut-off valves and disconnect from city power, water, and sewer and we would be good to go.

The next morning we moved to Woodland and after lunch drove the Cavalier to the Ariel store. Things hadn't changed a lot except for the interior of the store which had posted, I suspect, everything ever published about D. B. Cooper—Candi had been correct when she said I would be famous. In all likelihood this was fame I would never claim; I'd been in prison and I didn't like it in the least. The store was built for use as a chow hall for workers building the dam which now holds back Merwin Lake. It later served as a post office, among other things, before becoming the Ariel store. The next day we drove into Vancouver and located the house I hid in for two nights and the spot where I'd climbed out of the river. When Sue Ann asked why I was driving around a residential neighborhood I told her I was thinking about buying a house overlooking the river. She appeared to be getting bored so I stopped at Fort Vancouver for about an hour before crossing over the bridge and driving into downtown Portland. Sue Ann probably thought I was crazy when I stopped at a burger joint for dinner, but she didn't complain or ask any questions. My trip down memory lane was about over—the only thing left was the D. B. Cooper look-alike contest.

At a Salvation Army Thrift Store I purchased an outfit as close to the one I had worn when I boarded Northwest Orient flight 305 as I could find. When Sue Ann asked, "Do you intend to wear those clothes in public?"

"Yeah, I was looking for something kind of classy, what do you think?" She rolled her eyes, tilted her head, and looked at the ceiling without commenting.

I laughed and said, "I thought it would be a hoot to enter the D. B. Cooper look-alike contest. Do you think I'll win?" Again, she rolled her eyes without saying anything.

The day of the contest I mingled with other contestants at the store waiting for the judges' decision. In the meantime Sue Ann was looking at all the articles and pictures posted on the wall. She walked over, took me by the hand and asked, "Would you come over here for a minute?" I followed her to an area where the composite drawing circulated by the Feds and printed in every newspaper in the country shortly after the hijacking hung on a wall.

"Stand right here." I cooperated and put on a big smile, and then looked at the drawing pretending to study it for several seconds before turning back toward her and putting on a serious face as though imitating the expression of the person on the reward poster.

"Are you D. B. Cooper?"

"Yep," I responded.

"Seriously, are you really D. B. Cooper?"

"Absolutely, cross my heart and hope to die." I made the gesture with my finger while pretending to suppress a laugh but not quite able to pull it off.

I pointed to another look-alike contestant, "See the slight bulge just above his right hip?" I continued without waiting for her to respond, "That's a gun; the guy's a cop. I'll bet he comes to this little party every year because the Feds figure one day curiosity will get the best of old DB and he'll show up just to see what's going on. To their way of thinking a criminal always revisits the scene of his crime. Do you think if I were D. B. Cooper I'd be crazy enough to come to this shindig?"

"Well." she shrugged, arched her eyebrows, and said, "There are crazies out there, you know?"

Every one was pretty mellow by the time the judge made her choice and she didn't think I looked as much like DB as did Sue Ann, so I didn't fare too well in the contest. We hung around awhile, taking pictures and then left as the crowd started thinning out. On the way back to Woodland I started laughing and looked at Sue Ann. "What's so funny?" she asked.

"You started me thinking. I'll bet old DB has shown up for one of these contests. You'll probably never know, but he just may have been one of the contestants today. You might have met D. B. Cooper today."

"If he were to show up, do you think he would win?"

"Not likely." I started laughing again; there was an after-the-fact shot of adrenalin and I was a little intoxicated by my once-in-a-lifetime moment, and somewhat giddy.

She moved closer to me, reached over and gave me a little squeeze and said, "You are crazy."

"I know, but it keeps me from losing my mind." We both laughed.

"Where do you want to go from here?"

"It doesn't matter to me, what do you have in mind?"

"Nothing in particular; let's just get on the road and see where it takes us."

"Sounds good to me, let's do it."

I pulled off my D. B. Cooper outfit and threw it in the trash along with my memories and my fears; I would not revisit that part of my past again. There would be no lingering ghosts to haunt my dreams or wake me in the middle of the night.

Sue Ann stepped out of the shower, toweled herself dry, and asked as she slipped into bed, "Are you staying up all night?"

I smiled. I had a new lease on life. I was free to dream new and better dreams and I realized this really was the first day of the rest of my life. I was still smiling when I finished my shower and crawled into bed.

Sue Ann and I traveled about the country for more than four years and traveled through Texas several times; though I always stayed clear of the Panhandle, the desire to check on my parents grew each time I passed through the state until I found myself turning onto the gravel road leading to the ranch house where I grew up.

"Where are we going?"

"I thought I'd show you the old homestead; my father calls it Rancho Descanso. I thought I should spend a few days with my parents to see how they're doing and if they need anything. Is that okay with you?"

"Sure, I always liked the country. I grew up on a small farm, even had a pony. Do you have horses?"

"Used to; don't know about now. Working cowboys prefer ATVs and helicopters these days."

"That's terrible, why would anyone prefer ATVs to horses?"

"Well, to begin with, you don't have to saddle one before you head out to take care of the day's chores, you don't have to feed an ATV or clean up after it, or curry it down at the end of the day, they don't spook or wander away and leave you stranded when you get off to"—she cut me off in midsentence and obviously didn't like my answer.

"Okay, okay, I get the picture." She didn't say anything for a few minutes and then asked, "How far away is your ranch?"

"We've been driving through it since I turned off the blacktop."

"You're kidding!"

"Nope, not unless my dad sold it since I was here last."

"How long has it been since you saw your parents?"

"It's been well over ten years. I joined the navy right out of high school and haven't spent much time in these parts since I left home."

Sue Ann opened her mouth to speak, but either thought better of it or was distracted when I pulled to a stop in front of the house. Except for needing a new coat of paint, the place looked pretty good. I wasn't surprised to see my father sitting on the front porch. He always enjoyed sitting on the porch watching the sunset and often, especially when the moon was full, he'd remain outside well into the evening.

Sue Ann was a bit tentative as we stepped onto the porch.

"Hi, Pop, how you doing?"

"Oh, about as well as could be expected, I guess. How about you, son?"

"Well, I'm still walking and talking and breathing in and out, so I guess I'm doing okay. Pop, this is my friend Sue Ann."

"Pleased to meet you, young lady, how you doing?"

"Thank you, I'm doing well, sir."

"You two young'uns hitched?"

"No sir, we haven't talked about marriage, although it might not be a bad idea." I looked at Sue Ann as I spoke and she cocked her head and raised an eyebrow.

"Well, son, she's a good-looking filly. If I were you I'd think about putting a branding iron to her before she wanders over into some other man's pasture."

Sue Ann smiled and said, "Thank you for the nice compliment, sir." She continued with a bit of folksy talk I surmise she thought would appeal to my father. "I'm going over and rustle up some grub; would you like to join us for supper?"

"I'd be delighted to have supper with you, young lady." My father watched Sue Ann as she descended the porch steps and headed back toward the motor home and then turned to me and motioned to a chair, "Take a load off, son, and sit down."

I settled into the chair before I asked, "How's Ma?" I knew the answer before he spoke. A great sadness swept away his jovial mood. He looked away from me, perhaps to some distant time and place in his mind, or maybe just to keep me from seeing the tears glistening in the last rays of sunlight. It was several seconds before he turned and said, "Your mama had a heart attack back in the spring and died in the ambulance on the way to the hospital; there was nothing they could do for her."

"I'm sorry, Pop, I had no idea." There were other things I wanted to say, but I didn't know how or where to begin.

"I know." I knew there were things he wanted to say to me, as well, but figured they were better left unsaid. We sat looking out across the land for several minutes without speaking while watching the sun sink below the horizon. As a crimson rim began to glow on the distant hills he turned to me, slapped me on the knee and said, "Well, come on, boy, let's take a look at that camper of yours before it gets dark." It was as though he flipped a switch and put his grief behind a closed door, out of sight and out of mind. I explained several of the motor home's features as we walked around outside.

"Well son, it looks like you've done fairly well. What kind of business you in?"

"I dabble in real estate; it's been pretty good to me. It keeps me from working."

"Well, that's good; where do you live?"

"Under my hat. I've lived in this motor home for the last five years."

"You and the little lady?"

"Yes sir."

"You ever think about settling down?"

"Every now and then."

"You ever think about Texas?"

"It crosses my mind from time to time, and there have been occasions in my life when I wished I'd never left. I guess Texas is still in my blood."

"Well son, Texas is a good place to live as long as you stay away from the cities." Before I could respond Sue Ann opened the door and with another little folksy phrase announced, "Soup's on."

Sue Ann and my father hit it off from the beginning and during the ebb and flow of conversation over dinner my father ran the same questions past Sue Ann he'd asked me. By the time we finished eating he had her convinced she was a Texas girl who just happened to have been born in the wrong part of the country.

"Pop, Sue Ann was wondering if you had a horse she could ride." My father turned to Sue Ann and asked, "You ride much?"

"Not lately, but I used to ride a lot."

"Well I have little grey mare that would be just right for you. She's gentle and knows her way around the ranch. She doesn't spook easily and if you ever get lost just let her have her head and she'll bring you home safe and sound." He turned his attention to me,

"It'll be a great night for a ride; with a full moon and no breeze there's sure to be a lot of little critters out there talking to one another."

Sue Ann looked at me and said, "A moonlight ride sounds so romantic."

She turned back to my father and asked, "When should we get started?" Obviously I had nothing to say about it. She knew after that phrase, *sounds romantic*, I wasn't going to say no.

"Well, young lady, by the time I finish my coffee and another piece of your apple pie it'll be about time to saddle up Vientita. By then the moon should be well above the horizon and painting some mighty pretty pictures across the countryside." My father knew exactly what he was doing; he already knew I was considering hanging around, at least for a while, and he figured if he could sell Sue Ann on the idea of settling down here at Rancho Descanso I'd settle down with her. He was more right than he knew. It had been my hope that Candi would one day come to her senses and settle down with me in simple surroundings where we could live out our lives in peace and quiet and a reasonable amount of luxury—that was hoping beyond hope. On the other hand, Sue Ann was the flipside of Candi. She may not have been as exciting as Candi, but she was fun and easy to be with. She had a good head on her shoulders, could hold her own in any conversation on almost any subject and with anyone. She was refined, but didn't put on airs, and could be as down to earth as the situation demanded. She enjoyed the finer things in life, but was thrifty and knew the value of a dollar. She enjoyed our travels, but had hinted more than once her desire to settle down in a sparsely populated area, put simply, "in the middle of nowhere."

"Little Wind, is that Ma's horse? I'm surprised she's still around."

"It sure is, but it's not the same horse you remember. When your mama had to put her original mount out to pasture she named her next horse Vientita II, so this is actually Little Wind III."

Sue Ann had reservations about riding Little Wind; she was concerned about intruding on memories. My father told her my mother would be honored to have such a beautiful young lady riding Vientita.

While my father finished his pie and coffee Sue Ann and I slipped on boots and denims and then the three of us walked a couple of hundred yards to the stables, where Sue Ann was introduced to Little Wind. After the petting and nuzzling and baby talk, without asking for help or instructions, Sue Ann slipped a halter on her new friend, led her out into the breezeway, and tied her to the rail by the tack room. My father was impressed as Sue Ann chose a blanket and placed it on the mare's back and then eased a saddle onto the blanket, straightened it up and cinched it down, as she continued the baby talk.

"I used to ride my pony with nothing but a halter. Does she require a bridle?"

"My wife rode her with just a halter, but I would advise you to use a bridle until she gets to know you."

He turned his attention to me, "Well boy, have you forgotten how to saddle a horse?"

I laughed and said, "It has been a while, but I'm sure it'll come back to me."

"No doubt it will, so why don't you bring that chestnut gelding up here and show us what you haven't forgotten."

"Okay, what's his name?"

"I just call him Amigo."

While I threw a saddle on Amigo, cinched it down, and adjusted the stirrups, Sue Ann and my father talked in hushed tones. I could only guess, but I suspected my father was doing his best to convince Sue Ann she belonged in west Texas. I was about to swing into the saddle when my father said, "You may want to ride out to the canyon overlook. It's a little different than you remember; I fixed it up a bit."

To say he'd fixed it up a bit was an understatement. When I was a kid we'd spread our picnic on a big rock which served as both table and chairs; now there was a shelter built of rough-hewn timber. Two doors swung open on the canyon side, turning the shelter into a three-sided room. Moonlight flooded through the open doors and lit up the interior. Two comfortable-looking chairs with soft cushions sat on either side of a low table at one end of the shelter. The chairs faced the canyon, as did a porch swing at the other end. Chains attached to a rafter kept the swing about twenty inches off the floor. Along the wall behind the table and chairs stood a propane cookstove; various pots and pans along with dishes and flatware and an assortment of canned goods rested on shelves along the wall; a coffeepot sat on the stove. Behind the swing was a bed complete with sheets, blankets, and feather pillows. A propane lantern hung from a wire hook above the cookstove.

The moon floated above the rim and lit up the countryside as we sat swinging to and fro ever so slowly while looking at a star-studded west Texas sky and listening to sounds of the night. It was perhaps a half hour before either of us spoke. Finally, Sue Ann broke the silence.

"It's so peaceful out here; it's how I always pictured the West. When I was a little girl the local theater always showed western movies on Saturdays. I'd go to the matinee and then go home, get on my pony and pretend to be Dale Evans or Belle Starr or some other woman of the West, but mostly I pretended to be Dale Evans. I even named my pony Buttermilk."

"I'd forgotten about the quiet beauty I grew up with. As a youngster it was something I took for granted, and as a teenager my interests were at the opposite end of the scale. After my world turned upside down a few times I came to miss my ranching days and often wondered what life would have been like had I never left Texas. Someone once said, 'You can never go home.' But I think I can. I think I am home."

Sue Ann started to speak, then hesitated and fell silent. A minute or two passed before I asked, "Do you think you could be happy living out here with no shopping malls or beauty salons, with the closest neighbor 10 miles away?"

She snuggled closer and said, "I'm happy now, why do you ask?"

"Well, Pop is getting on in years. He's all alone now, and I'd kind of like to stay around and look after him, and I'd like for you to stay with me."

"Are you proposing to me?"

"Yeah, I guess I am."

"I've been wondering for the last couple of years why you hadn't brought up the subject of marriage. I even dropped a hint every now and then. I was beginning to think there was something wrong with me."

"What would you have said had I asked you to marry me a year or two ago?"

"I'd have said yes."

"What about now?"

She slipped her arms around my neck, touched her lips to mine for a moment and said, "I haven't changed my mind." As time passed and nature took its course we moved from the swing to the bed.

We rode back to the barn without talking; there was nothing left to say. We watered the horses before leading them into the stables. We were still silent when we stopped at the tack room and removed their saddles. After we brushed the horses down with currycombs we led them back to their stalls and tossed them some hay. Outside the barn Sue Ann slipped her arm in mine as we strolled toward the motor home. We were approaching the house before she broke the silence and asked, "When are you going to tell your father?"

"In the morning."

We were just passing the front porch when a voice from the darkness asked, "You young'uns have a good ride?"

Sue Ann leaned close and whispered, "I don't think you should wait until morning."

I whispered back, "Are you trying to get me on record?"

She giggled and said, "Maybe."

We walked up to the porch and while I was trying to figure out just what to say, Sue Ann responded, "We had an incredible ride, sir."

"Did you ride out to the canyon?"

Sue Ann was still carrying the conversation, "Yes sir, we did. It's beautiful out there. I love the little house you built."

I figured I'd better get it over with. I knew he would have a lot of questions. I also knew he'd wait until morning—he wouldn't ask his first question until we finished breakfast and he had his second cup of coffee in hand.

"Pop, what if I told you Sue Ann and I were thinking about getting married and settling down around here?"

"That would make me very happy, son, very happy indeed."

The end

Epilogue

If you find yourself in a west Texas restaurant and notice an old dude in faded denims sitting across from a knockout blonde, stop over and wish me well. If you address me as DB I'll pretend you are crazy, but you might be the recipient of a knowing smile. Although my wife won't answer to Sue Ann—surely you didn't think I would give the feds any help in finding me—she does have a southern name; listen for the accent.

You might find Sue Ann shopping at Neiman Marcus or see me trying on boots at the Branding Iron. I might be the guy riding the old Knucklehead Harley you just passed. I may be a neighbor hosting the community Fourth of July barbeque you're attending. Or I might be the politician you voted for in a local election. Sue Ann may be one of the entertainers at a summer's evening concert on the green.

You might bump into us line dancing or see us cheering on a couple of young barrel racers at the local rodeo. You may have talked with us in the checkout line at the grocery store or shook hands with us in church last Sunday. However, it is highly unlikely you will ever see me, Texas is a big state, but on the other hand, you just might.

Yes, I still look over my shoulder from time to time.

DB Cooper